SLOCUM LOOKED AT
LUMBAR'S MASSIVE ARMS
AND KNEW HE DIDN'T
STAND MUCH OF A CHANCE

Slocum worked to stay out of Lumbar's reach. There was a sharp pain in his shoulder, but he ignored it and threw punches aimed at Lumbar's nose. He laid a rabbit punch against Lumbar's neck, followed up with hard slaps against his ears. He maneuvered himself into position and smashed another sledgehammer punch into the nose. Around and around, back and forth Slocum danced, all the while hammering at Lumbar's ears and nose, until it looked as if the blows were all that kept the man from falling. Then Slocum backed off to just the right distance and kicked with all his might, his foot catching Lumbar in the balls.

JAKE LOGAN

SLOCUM'S FIRE

PLAYBOY PRESS
PAPERBACKS

For DICK SHARP—
His love for the Old West
remains so strong,
he's yet to quit
talking to horses.

SLOCUM'S FIRE

Cover illustration by Bart Jerner.

Copyright © 1979 by Playboy.

Published simultaneously in the United States and Canada by Playboy Press, Chicago, Illinois. Printed in the United States of America. Library of Congress Catalog Card Number: 78-62020. First edition.

Books are available at quantity discounts for promotional and industrial use. For further information, write our sales-promotion agency. Ventura Associates, 40 East 49th Street, New York, New York 10017.

ISBN: 0-872-16507-8

On the night of October 8, 1871, a fire broke out in Chicago that has come to be known as the Great Chicago Fire. Three hundred people were killed; there was approximately 200 million dollars in property damage.

There was another fire that same night. It began in a small logging town in Wisconsin called Peshtigo. That fire quickly spread from the town to burn large areas of Wisconsin and Upper Michigan. Nobody has ever been able to estimate its damage in terms of dollars. Thirteen hundred people were killed; 1,280,000 acres of forest were destroyed.

1

"It's a hundred-thousand-dollar job, John. Our biggest job ever."

"So you say, Curly." Slocum hunkered at the edge of the campfire, idly chucking pebbles into the coals as he listened to Curly Boyle chatter about tomorrow's job. "So you say." He glanced across the clearing to where Dorsey, Curly's latest partner, sat crouched between the roots of a tree.

"Mebbe more money 'n that, John. One hundred fifty thousand mebbe," insisted Curly. The bald crown of his head bobbed up and down as he talked. He was excited; his wide, squinty eyes were seeing a rich future. "All depends on how many miners they got to pay off." His tongue clucked inside his chinless jaws and a tone of querulous righteousness entered his voice. "The mine only pays them poor miners ev'ry other month. Oh, it's slave conditions, John, 'ceptin' a man who hires on in April, he ain't goin' to quit afore June. No, sir! He'll stay put and wait his pitiable wages. Over two hun'erd of them poor fellers. It's like I always said, John, you just cain't get rich workin' for somebody."

They were camped near a river. Tall pines surrounded them. The river was still full with the spring thaw. It rushed past its banks, splashing over rocks with an easy rhythm. The night was warm and would have been pleasant if mosquitoes hadn't been buzzing thick as midday flies.

Slocum crumbled a twig in his hand, tossed it into the fire and watched it burst into flame. The job didn't feel right to him, and Curly's constant chattering was beginning to get on his nerves. It was Curly who came up with the original plan for the job. Curly wasn't known for keen thinking. A nervy bastard, good in a fight, a fine man to share a good time with but, he just tended to confuse his balls with his brains. Still, this was the best plan Slocum had ever heard come from Curly.

He had been going through a dry spell when Curly approached him with it. The soles of his boots were about as thick as the seat of his pants, and one-third of a hundred thou would buy a hell of a wardrobe. So he had reluctantly agreed to come in on the job. But only after Curly had agreed to drop his "de-version'ry tactic" of throwing sticks of dynamite as they rode out of town.

"Joe Didion's sheriff of Ora Grande, Curly," Slocum had told him. "We're not blowing up his town. Or shooting his people."

"Wouldn't hurt Joe for the world, John. But you know we might have to do some shootin'."

"If we do, then we're in trouble already. We ride out the same way we ride in. Slow."

"However you say, John," Curly had responded, turning the leadership over to Slocum. "You're still my major. It's how I always look at you."

"We hit the reins when we pass the last house in town. Ride hard to where we'll have fresh horses staked. Split our shares on the spot. Ride our separate ways."

Slocum's main objection was Curly's new sidekick. The job needed three men, but Dorsey was still a kid. Wet behind the ears and cocky as a two-month-old rooster in a house of old hens. He wore a pile of long blond hair, which, Slocum figured, was why Curly had started riding with him.

Again Slocum glanced across to where Dorsey crouched. He frowned at what he saw. The boy was dreamily spinning the wheel of a spur. Mosquitoes buzzed unnoticed near his round, pale cheeks. He might have been thinking about tomorrow's job. He could

8

just as easily have been lost in the steady whirring noise of the spinning spur.

"No need for you to frown and scowl, John," Curly laughed. "Dorsey 'n me've hit three banks. Nary a problem. Ain't that right, Dorsey?"

Dorsey grunted in answer. His features so lacked expression that Slocum wondered if the kid had even heard the question.

"Those were sod town banks you and Dorsey hit," said Slocum. "Bet you didn't pull more than a couple thousand out of a one."

"That's just the damn point, John. I cain't take no more sod town banks."

Curly was rubbing on his most recently discovered hair restorer, an oily black substance that dully reflected the flames from the fire. He didn't have so much as one strand of hair since he was five years old, but he continued trying every quack cure-all that came his way. He never wore a hat, no matter what the season, because he believed the "nat'ral elements" would fertilize his scalp. Then he'd turn around and grease his head with the most unnatural concoctions. He was a mass of contradictions. Hot tempered one moment, soft-spoken the next. His blue flannel shirt was so dark with grime it looked a part of the night, yet all the buttons were fastidiously buttoned, and a wild spring poppy peeked out of a buttonhole. His idea of a bath was to drench himself with a four-bit bottle of general store cologne, yet he would have nothing to do with smoking or chewing tobacco because he considered it bad for the breath. He went pie-eyed crazy in a whorehouse but stuttered when he came within ten yards of a "dee-cent" woman.

"Through with sod town banks, John. An' with all the rest of it." Curly spoke with a plaintive insistence. "Cain't take no more lookin' over my shoulder wherever I ride. This job's it for me. The stake for the rest of my life. Think I'd bring in Dorsey if I di'nt have faith in him? Think I'd do that?"

9

Slocum wasn't convinced. "It's a high pressure job. Lot of seasoned men would crack under the pressure of the money we're going for."

"Don't let his purty corn-color hair fool you. Dorsey's got the grit."

Slocum slapped a mosquito. "I'm taking your word, Curly." He laughed lightly. "Who knows? Maybe his apple-cheek freshness will stop people from looking close at your more familiar features."

The black hair restorer had given Curly's head the appearance of a greased cannonball. He gave his head a final little pat and said, "If I wear a hat, nobody'll rec'nize me from them post office pictures."

Dorsey snickered. "What about your gimpy legs? No hat can hide the way you walk. Or cover up the fact you don't got a chin in your jaw."

Curly ignored Dorsey's remarks. He picked up a gritty cork from the ground and carefully rubbed all the dirt from it onto his shirt. He started to cork his bottle of hair restorer, took a different notion and brought the bottle to his nose and sniffed. His features twisted suspiciously. "Damn, John. This smells just like what some thievin' dentist down in Lincoln County sold me once."

"Try drinking it," Slocum said. "Maybe it'll grow something on your chest."

"Di'nt that time. But—" He put the bottle to his lips and tipped it up. A second later he leaped to his feet, gagging and clutching his throat. He spat what he hadn't swallowed into the fire. Flames hissed and shot up five feet into the air.

Slocum laughed as Curly continued to spit and sputter. Dorsey's full lips curved into an odd smile. He looked more disgusted than amused.

"Good God in heaven!" Curly managed to mutter. "I think I found the right one, John. Anything tastes that bad'll grow somethin'."

Dorsey snickered, "Grow you right into a grave, you old fart."

Slocum reached inside his saddlebags and brought

10

out a bottle of whiskey. As he threw the bottle to Curly, he said, "Here. Clear your throat." He reached again into the saddlebags and pulled out the rolled-up sketches of the Ora Grande bank and the town layout. He unrolled the sketches and moved closer to the light of the fire to examine them once again. He knew them by heart by this time, knew every line, but he still wasn't satisfied.

"Now I know what you're a-thinkin', John. But we couldn't ride in there an' risk Joe Didion spottin' us. Now that's a fact. Dorsey's the only one could do it. Didion don't know him. Ain't them drawin's Dorsey made near to perfect? Ain't they?"

"They're still drawings."

"Worth a hundred thousand dollars. Them fellers who draw the presidents on the dollars, they never made near that much money." He drank deeply from the bottle. "This ain't very good whiskey, John."

"Don't drink it."

Curly made no move to give up the bottle. "After tomorrow, you'll be able to afford better. Thought yet what you'll do with your share?"

Slocum reached out and broke a cloud of mosquitoes that was circling near him. "I'll wait 'til I get it before spending it."

"Got me some good plans." Curly gazed up at the sky. The night was full of stars and he looked like he was about to reach up and grab one. "Yes, sir! Good plans. Be pleased to have you join me, John. Ever think 'bout Frisco? Big town, new start. Mebbe we could git on a boat 'n go to one o' them islands. Never been on an ocean."

A mild breeze was moving up from the river. Slocum picked up his bowie knife; he walked into the woods and cut a few pine boughs. He returned to the clearing and added the green wood to the fire, hoping it would create enough smoke to scatter the damn mosquitoes.

Dorsey hadn't moved from his position at the tree, but he had stopped playing with his spur. He'd found a length of twine and now he was involved with making cat's cradles.

Slocum stood staring into the fire. "Wonder why nobody ever thought of this job before?"

"Dammit!" Curly's voice was sharp and sour. "We been through all this! Since when do you have last-minute jitters? Ain't like you!"

"You're the one who's sounding jittery all of a sudden. I'm just thinking out loud." The pine boughs had begun to smother the fire. Slocum kicked them and opened a little air for the flames. "Can't help but think others might have gotten the same idea. Dropped it when they learned Joe Didion was sheriff of Ora Grande. Joe's a tough man. A well-liked one, too."

"Now don't I know that? Don't you and I and Joe go back a long ways?" Curly lurched to his feet. He had a pair of stunted legs—the result of the same childhood disease that had left him hairless—and he stomped crab-wise around the fire. He ground his teeth, kicking out at pebbles. Slocum noticed how near to empty the bottle was. "We're hittin' the bank in Joe's town," Curly continued. "Think I like it? Think I'd be doin' it if it weren't necessary? It's gonna be a smirch on him. Damned if I like it!"

"We're riding in a few hours." Slocum took the bottle. "You've had enough to drink."

"Damn right we're ridin'." He leaned close to Slocum, his chinless jaw working furiously. "My last job, John. Don't you take it lightly!" He spun around and dropped to his heels. He grabbed a stick and poked up red sprays of sparks from the fire.

Slocum quietly said, "Let's get some rest."

"Cain't take the life no more, John." Curly sounded as if something had caught in his throat. "It ain't that I lost my nerve. I jus' cain't stand it no more." The end of his stick had taken fire. He held it near his face and stared deeply at its flame. "Frisco. New start. First off, I'll stop in that whorehouse for a week. Madame Lu's. Mebbe two weeks. Then I'm goin' to invest. Store of

12

some kind. Gunsmith, mebbe. Nobody better 'n me with guns. Or mebbe just a saloon. Or a goddamn feed store. I'd be pleased if you'd come in with me, John."

"A city's not for me, Curly." Slocum chuckled. "Hell, if what I hear's true 'bout that Madame Lu's, you'll be fucked blind and broke in a week."

Curly stabbed his stick into the ground. He twisted on his heels and his squinty eyes met Slocum's. His voice was a gruff whisper. "We could get us a spread somewheres. We'll have money 'nough for a nice piece of land. Good start on a herd. We could buy us some o' them foreign bulls. Breed our own strain. Think of it. Our own strain o' beef."

Slocum nodded. He felt suddenly warm, as if the skin of his face had somehow tightened. "It's a thought," he said.

Curly's hands came up and struggled to shape words. "All our lives, John, we've had to play what's been dealt us. It's all been shit. The war. Christ knows that neither of us shoulda survived Shiloh. You tried goin' back home. Look what you got. Me, I had no home to go to. Sherman saw to that. We got dealt this goddamn outlaw trail, John. Dealer's holdin' the fuckin' percentage. How many fellers we know who're dead? How much longer we got? After tomorrow we can start dealin' our own game, John. It's never been done before."

"Joe Didion did it. Joe plays his own game."

Curly sprang to his feet. His hands balled into tight fists looking to punch something. "Joe's a fool! Makes fifty goddamn dollars a month. Ev'ry Saturday he has to fight drunk cowboys 'n hope nobody shoots him in the back. Has himself three brat kids. A woman who used to spread her legs fer more 'n his salary. A goddamn fool!"

Slocum lifted the whiskey bottle. "Maybe." He wet his dry throat.

"No maybe's! And after we rob his bank, he won't even have his fuckin' fifty a month. Voters'll git rid o' him. His woman'll be spreadin' her legs again to feed the brats. Joe, he'll be on this outlaw trail again. Else he'll be a drunk. Cleanin' spittoons while his wife fucks in a back room." He clutched his stomach, looking about to fall. Suddenly, he grabbed the whiskey away from Slocum and stumbled into the woods.

Slocum slowly got to his feet. Curly had disappeared into the darkness, but Slocum could hear him staggering toward the river.

Dorsey snickered. "He's like that 'fore ev'ry job we ever done. He's who you should worry 'bout. Not me."

Slocum slowly crossed until he stood above where Dorsey lay. "Why's that, Dorsey?"

The kid had just completed a cat's cradle. He stretched it tight. "He's a worn-out old prick is why."

Slocum looked down at Dorsey. The mesh of the cat's cradle masked the kid's full-lipped sneer. Slocum wanted to kick the kid a hard one in the ribs, but a kid with broken ribs couldn't ride. "You're a kid, Dorsey. You still play with a kid's string game. If you ever manage to grow up, I just might listen to your opinion about a man like Curly Boyle. But until that time, you keep your mouth shut around me."

Slocum turned and started in the direction that Curly had taken. Dorsey called out, "Maybe I'll want to talk to you tomorrow, Slocum. After the job."

Slocum continued on out of the clearing. He slowly walked between the tall pines and down the rather steep slope leading to the river. Curly was leaning against a tree at the river's edge when Slocum found him.

"Going to be able to ride, Curly?"

"How come it got so cold, John?" Curly shivered, though the air wasn't chilly. Slocum couldn't tell whether the man's shivering was due to drink or to the jitters.

Slocum smiled. "River winds, friend."

"Couldn't do it alone, John. Somehow with you it don't seem so hard. Job's easy enough. Joe's what makes it hard."

14

Slocum took the bottle. There wasn't much left in it. He drank the remainder and threw the bottle into the river. Then he reached out and put a firm hand against Curly's thin shoulder and pushed him in the water.

"It'll sober you up, Curly."

Curly surfaced with a shriek. The shock of the icy spring water kept him from speaking. His hair restorer dripped oily black streaks down the lines of his face.

"You look like a shivering walnut," laughed Slocum. He wouldn't let Curly crawl back up the bank. "You need the bath. Joe Didion would've smelled you a mile outside of his town."

"Ch—Ch—Christ, John." Curly stood in water up to his waist, flapping his arms and slapping himself for warmth. "Did, did you have to be so fu—fu—fuckin' drastic."

2

They stopped the payroll guards about two miles outside of town. There were two mounted men; a third drove the wagon. They made them strip to their underwear and tied them to a tree. Then they put on the guards' uniforms.

"Collect their boots, Dorsey," ordered Slocum. "Give each one a swallow of water."

Dorsey sullenly did what he was told. He hadn't spoken a word all morning.

"Just in case you men get yourselves untied," Slocum told the guards, "we don't want you walking too fast. We'll leave your boots down the road a piece."

One of the guards spoke. "You boys can't get away with this. Let us loose 'n we'll fergit the whole thing."

Slocum turned his Colt on the man who spoke. "Since you're speaking for the rest, where's your authorization?"

"Don't know what you're talkin' 'bout."

"We're a bit rushed." Slocum planted a shot an inch away from one of the man's feet. "In ten seconds, I start shooting off your toes."

It took five seconds. "The wagon seat."

Slocum climbed into the wagon. He found what he wanted stuck to a clipboard: the company's authorization order for the bank to turn over the payroll. The single page order was simply written and presented no new problems. He nodded to Curly and Dorsey and they headed for Ora Grande.

Slocum drove the wagon. It clattered and was very uncomfortable to sit in. It wasn't much more than a buckboard fitted with a steel cage. There was no key to the cage; the guards weren't allowed to carry one. If all went well, the Ora Grande banker would unlock the cage after accepting their authorization. They would load the payroll and the cage would be re-locked. When they had gotten themselves safely out of town, they would use one of Curly's dynamite sticks on the wagon. A noisy but effective key.

The wagon didn't ride easily. Slocum cushioned his ass against a wadded-up horse blanket. Once they neared town, he would have to throw aside the blanket and crouch low. Joe Didion wasn't likely to recognize a slouched down, round-shouldered driver as John Slocum.

Curly kept his mount close to the wagon. His bald head was hidden under a guard's cap. He chattered steadily but, fortunately for Slocum's peace of mind, the wagon's noise swallowed most of what Curly said.

Dorsey rode slightly ahead of them. His hair hung low, a sharp yellow contrast against the guard's blue cap and shirt. It bounced against his shoulders. A few times he reached back to flounce it or he pushed a hand beneath it and made a great show of squeezing a stiff neck.

"Ain't it pretty, John." Curly was amused. His gloomy mood from last night had passed and he wasn't suffering any hangover effects. "Dorsey thinks

16

he's funnin' me. Oh, I wants me some long yella hair like that, 'cept I wants it attached to a nekkid woman. Yes, sir! An' I been thinkin'. When I get to Frisco, I just might buy me some store-bought hair."

Dorsey held his horse in check and waited for them to reach him. He didn't look Slocum in the eye when he spoke. "Why settle for the payroll? There's a whole bank to clean out."

"Now I explained that, youngster," chuckled Curly. He became an indulgent elder repeating a lesson to a slow youth. "We ain't bank robbers. We're just payroll guards pickin' up a payroll."

"I say we should take it all," Dorsey grumbled.

"Ora Grande bank ain't all that big, Dorsey," continued Curly. "Ten, mebbe twenty thousand. We take it, they gonna know what we are. Even if we git out of town, Joe Didion's gonna have a posse on our tail in two quick blinks. No sense riskin' the payroll for a dinky ten thousand."

"I cased that sleepy town," whined Dorsey. "We can outshoot, outride the bunch."

"You can't beat Joe Didion, kid," Slocum said quietly.

Dorsey reached into his saddlebag and pulled out a stick of dynamite. "Your old pal Didion. He can't beat this."

Slocum moved like lightning. He stood up in the wagon seat and slapped Dorsey hard. The kid dropped the dynamite and almost fell out of his saddle. "You got any more sticks with you, drop 'em now," Slocum said.

Dorsey wiped a streak of blood from his lip. "How we goin' to blow the goddamn cage?"

"Curly?" Slocum asked. "How many sticks you got?"

"One, John. Just like you said."

Slocum started at Dorsey.

"Whatever you say, Slocum." Dorsey pulled out four sticks and threw them away. Slocum continued to stare until he pulled out two more.

"Get this straight, kid," said Slocum. "You don't

have to worry about Didion. You do anything to upset this operation, I'll kill you on the spot."

Dorsey sucked his split lip. "When the job's all done. I maybe'll want to have a few words with you."

"Fine." Slocum's mouth curved into a tight smile. "Then Curly and I'll divide the take two ways 'stead of three."

Dorsey snickered and rode on ahead.

"Now do me a favor, John." Curly clucked his tongue. "Don't shoot him 'less you have to. A good boy. Jus' needs a little time."

Slocum slapped the reins. He wanted a smoke but he'd used the last of his makings two nights ago.

"So what do you think of my idea, John?"

"What idea?" Slocum asked without interest and knowing full well Curly would tell him anyway.

"Me buyin' some store-bought hair in Frisco?"

"Reason you don't have hair, Curly, is you didn't jerk off enough when you were a kid."

"I'm serious, John. Some store hair, a fancy suit, low heel city boots. Mebbe a walkin' stick 'n I can say my legs was a war injury. Be all slick as snot when I walk into Madame Lu's Palace o' Pleasure. Yes, sir! I'll start by playin' a little roulette, shake the dice, an' then . . . oh sweet madame!" He rolled the name around his tongue like he was tasting it. "Lu. Madame Lu. Don't that place of her's sound like somethin' we deserve? Don't it, John? What you think she is? Chinee? Or Japanee?

"I heard Comanche."

Curly slapped his leg and laughed. "Wonder what she charges for the French way? Hell, I'm a-goin' to pay it. I figure the few of us poor fellers who survived what we survived deserve it all. Sort of in the line of reparations. You an' me survivin' Marsden's Treachery there at Corinth. In a just world, John, we'd be given least a free week. Hell of a note when you have to pay for what's due you. You ever kill Marsden like you said you would?"

Slocum's mouth became hot and dry. *Marsden.* Slocum felt the flare of an old and bitter hate.

"Did you, John? Did you kill him?"

"Not yet." His voice was low and gruff. "Still waiting to run into him."

"Mebbe with your money, you could mebbe hire the Pinkertons to help you run him down. I know how he's always been a ripe boil on your butt. Marvelous thing, money. Know what I heard, John? There's a floor in Madame Lu's where the women puts on these shows. Get themsel's all dressed up. Horse costumes, sailor suits, stiff white collars, anythin' you can think of. A man don' necessarily jus' watch. Say you always had this itch to be an admiral. You'd dress like one and be in your cabin, way I hears it, and they got a way o' makin' the cabin just like at sea. An' the door opens, see, 'n there's this cabin boy, eh, girl. Course none o' this is to my taste, John, but I sure would like to—"

Curly's chattering blended with the clatter of the wagon. Slocum concentrated on the reins, first letting them go slack, then snapping them taut. The wheels rolled over deep dry ruts and sometimes seemed to shake the earth out from under. The horses kicked back dust that coated his face and entered his nostrils like cold ash. The wheels rolled and smashed like small explosions, taking his mind back to the war, to Shiloh, where he'd first met Curly Boyle and Joe Didion— back to the events of Marsden's Treachery.

3

SHILOH, TENNESSEE, APRIL 6, 1862.

The fighting began at dawn on a bright, clear Sunday. Within 48 hours, 23,000 men would be dead.

Major John Slocum's battalion was among the first to charge. His men were a close, tight-knit group. They shared the kinship of having grown up in the same hilly

19

area of the South. They'd been shooting straight since childhood, and honor was something they'd been taught to fight for.

The Federals were dispersed into three main bodies. They were in a three-way box. Swampy bogs or rivers cut off any possible Yankee retreat, and the long line of the Confederate attack made up the fourth wall of the box. By noon, the Yanks had been inexorably pushed together. The noise of bursting explosions and whining shells, and the cries of the wounded were all but swallowed by the shrill shouting of rebel yells as the Confederates charged for what was thought to be the final charge of the battle.

But the Yankees stood their ground, firing so heavily that within an hour the battle site was known as the "Hornet's Nest."

Slocum quickly lost what amounted to a full company of men. By mid-afternoon he had no idea how many of his men were left, nor where most of them were. There was no longer a battle plan, nor the time to mount one. Senior officers would appear and give him conflicting orders. The only clear thing was the need to take the Hornet's Nest. Time and again he tried to mass the soldiers around him, only to have them scattered by a volley of Federal shots.

Late in the day a shell blew his horse out from under him. He managed to swing his feet clear of the stirrups and fall safely away before the dead weight of his horse caught him. As he crawled to his feet, he grasped the arm of another fallen soldier and attempted to help him. Then he saw the dark hole in the man's stomach and the insignia on the shoulder boards.

"General John—" he started to say.

"Go on, lad." The general gripped at the pain that was killing him. "Go on."

"We will," promised Slocum.

He pushed away the general's stiffening dead hands. He stood up and walked away. He left with rage, kicking aside anything or anybody in his way.

20

He suddenly found himself in hand-to-hand combat with three Yankees. His bayonet broke in the belly of one. He knocked a second Yank down with his fist and was reaching for his side arm when he was pushed from behind. He was twisting around ready to fire the pistol even as he hit the ground, when he realized the push had saved him from a Yankee saber. He saw a bandy-legged, bald man break the saber swinger's skull with a musket butt. Then, as the Yank Slocum had knocked down struggled to stand, the bald man skewered him with a bayonet.

The bald man wore no uniform. His clothing was torn and stained with blood. He took hold of Slocum and lifted him to his feet.

"Boyle. Georgia Volunteers." He grinned. "Don't offen git to knock down of'cers."

Ten feet in front of them, a blue uniform stood up from a gully. Slocum fired a shot. The uniform dropped.

"Where's your outfit, Boyle?"

"I 'spect heaven 'r hell."

A volley of shell burst around them. They hit the ground.

"Confederate shells," said Slocum. "Or else the Yankees are firing on themselves."

"In any case, sir, I suggest a strategic ree-treat."

The South never took the Hornet's Nest. They managed to surround it. The end of the first day's battle was considered a Confederate victory, but nobody celebrated it. It had cost too much.

Somehow, maybe crazy luck, Major Slocum and the bald Georgia Volunteer made it back to their own lines. It was evening. The air was thick and tired and gray. They eased their weary bodies against the wheel of an abandoned Yank supply wagon.

"You're a hell of a fighting man, Boyle," Slocum said after catching his breath.

"Thank you sir. If it's all the same, sir, could you call me Curly? Prefer it to Boyle. Had a bad case o'

21

boils as a kid. Hurt like the blazes 'n my rightful name always brings 'em to mind."

A fog of fumes and smoke lay over the wrecked ground. The wagon they had slumped against was within hearing distance of where the surgeons had hoisted the bloody shirt that signalled an aid station. Cries of the wounded cut the gray air.

"Where's your uniform, Curly?" Slocum asked.

"Ain't been issued one. Had to damn near shoot me a quartermaster to get me ammunition. We ain't the most organized army in history." His odd, chinless features twisted into a friendly grin. "Now I'll be off to find my outfit. Been a pleasure fightin' with you, sir." The knees of his runty legs looked like the points of triangles headed in opposite directions. He turned and started walking in a third direction.

"Curly!" Slocum stopped him. "It's customary to salute officers in this army."

"Beg pardon, sir." Curly turned and raised his hand in a half salute. "Us Georgia boys, we don' consider us part o' the army, such as it is. We volunteered to fight Yankees."

"Weren't many of you boys here today. Doubt if many are left. Think you can learn the basic regulations? I'll arrange for you to join my battalion."

"Oh, I know the rules. An' you're a good man. Wouldn't mind takin' orders from you, major."

"We need men like you." Slocum smiled. "Hope to hell I don't have to hang you for insubordination."

Slocum had less than two companies left. He gathered his men and saw to it they got full rations. Many were in pain from untreated wounds. Whiskey was found—Slocum didn't ask from where—and those with Yankee shots in their arms and legs were fed whiskey enough to withstand the probe of a sharpened bayonet. Every man knew it was better to be doctored by a comrade than be trusted to the barbers who were calling themselves surgeons. Mangled fingers and hands were amputated at the joints and cauterized with fire. Oozing

22

wounds were packed with gun powder, and wet tobacco was used as a poultice on burns and lesions. A broth of boiled tobacco, sweetened with molasses and laced with whiskey, was fed to the feverish.

It was nearly midnight when Slocum went to command headquarters. He came upon a group of officers sitting around a fire. They were a cheerless, quiet group, with a number of them obviously fighting to stay awake.

"No point going further, John," one said. "We're all here same as you. Wondering what to expect in the morning." He pointed his thumb over his shoulder. "Over yonder the generals are still arguing about today."

Slocum glanced in the direction of the command tent. He saw the moving silhouettes of the generals inside and heard their muffled, angry shouts. "General Johnson never allowed this," said Slocum. He squatted at the fire and accepted a cup of coffee and a cigar. "Who's our new commander?"

"That's what they're shouting about. From what we can hear, Bragg or Beauregard look like the choice. Major-General Marsden is the one you hear makin' the loudest noise."

"Doesn't make sense." Slocum held up his cup for a shot of the passing bottle. "Beauregard's next in command."

"We are not at West Point any more, John," someone said. "Chain of command here is about as tight as a whore's cunt."

"Who's Marsden?" asked Slocum.

The men around the fire laughed. One said, "He's what's known as a friend of a friend of Jeff Davis. He arrived 'bout five minutes after the end of the battle and demanded to be put in charge."

"He's an engineer," said someone else. "Least that's 'bout all we've managed to hear of his qualifications. An engineer and some kind of lay preacher. 'Pears God is on the side of the Confederate States of America, but only, according to Major-General Marsden, if

23

Major-General Marsden carries our cross of victory."

Slocum closed his ears to their talk. Camp gossip never interested him. He finished his coffee and wandered away from the fire, idly puffing his cigar.

Eventually, he found himself at the top of a hill. Not a big hill, but high enough. He saw clearly the Union fires across the way. Tomorrow night, he thought, we'll be warming ourselves over there, or they'll be here. He lay down. The grass was damp and its fresh smell was welcome. He closed his eyes, and without meaning to, fell asleep.

The sound of a fast-ridden horse brought him awake. The horse was nearly on him. It reared back as its rider pulled the reins. Slocum, still groggy from his nap, was slow to react and the horse's hooves narrowly missed him.

"Soldier! What are you doing up here?"

The voice boomed from a huge, barrel-chested man. He wore the uniform of a Confederate officer. A custom-made uniform with many extra buttons, a plumed hat and enough braid to lasso the moon.

Slocum saluted. "Major Slocum, sir."

"Didn't see your insignia, Major," the man cut in, returning the salute. "Is it the darkness? Or is your uniform out of order?"

"My uniform got torn up today, sir."

"As did all of the Confederacy, Major." The man's thick hands looked pale and soft in the moonlight. He placed them on his saddle horn and leaned heavily toward Slocum. His shoulders were an awesome size. His bulk blocked the sky from Slocum's view. "General Johnson, may he rest in peace, did not know how to command. As God is my witness I make that statement. You agree, Major?"

Slocum said nothing.

"I'm Major-General Marsden. Goddammit! When I ask a question, I get an answer, Major."

"I thought General Johnson a good man, sir."

"His goodness is the concern of God, not me. He

24

did not know how to command. The Federals were divided. He pushed them together and gave them unity. That isn't strategy, Major. You know about strategy, Major?"

"I was at West Point, sir."

"Then may I assume you agree with me when I say we should be on the attack now. God gave us a victory today despite Johnson's stupidity. We should be taking advantage of that victory instead of giving the enemy the night to reorganize."

Slocum stated the obvious. "Our troops are too exhausted to mount a night attack."

"The enemy's tired, too, Major. God gives strength to those who believe in Him. He gives no strength to cowards. He causes His wrath to fall upon those who shun Him. The South has shunned Him this night, as I have been shunned, Major. I came to lead victories, not oversee craven retreats. Beauregard has refused me my rightful place of command. He has already made plans for tomorrow's retreat. A shameful situation."

Marsden removed his plumed hat and wiped his forehead with a handerchief. He glanced at the distant Union campfires and continued. "Major, this all sticks in my craw. I've half a notion to swing my horse right and go over to those Yankees instead of heading on back to Montgomery. They're not packing up to retreat."

He put his hat back on his head. "God have mercy on the South, Major. God have mercy."

Marsden slapped his horse and rode away.

Slocum headed back to his men. Behind him he heard the fading sound of Marsden's galloping horse.

APRIL 7, 1862

General Beauregard took over Johnson's command. His decision was to hold their position through the day, then use the cover of darkness to fall back to Corinth.

Slocum ordered his men to dig in and get ready. Their morale was low. They complained and grumbled a great deal. The story of Marsden went up and down the whole of the Confederate lines, and it bitterly rankled the men. Slocum made no mention of his encounter with Marsden, but the story the men told closely paralleled what Marsden had so loudly told him. The man had appeared shortly after the first day's battle and demanded to lead a suicidal night attack on the Yanks. When he didn't get what he wanted, he declared the South was lost, climbed on his horse and headed back to Montgomery.

Once the attack began, the men were too busy for further complaints or gossip. There was simply no stopping Grant's army. No sooner would the rebels knock down a line of blue than another line would appear. By mid-afternoon it was clear to all they could hold no longer. The order came down to retreat.

Corinth was twenty miles away. Slocum's men and about two hundred others marched the right flank of the retreat. The terrain was such that as they neared Corinth they had to swing wide of their main forces and pass through a narrow, mile long place that hadn't a name on the map. There were broad hills on either side, but the hills were too low to properly call the place a valley. Halfway through they were hit by a crossfire of cannon.

The air screamed; the earth burst beneath them. They had no way to fight back; the cannon were out of range of their weapons. They ran. They stumbled and fell and picked each other up and ran.

Slocum picked up a fallen man. He didn't know it was Curly Boyle until he heard Curly say, "Save ya'self, Major."

A shell exploded near them. The impact threw Slocum and Curly down. Slocum's head banged hard against a rock, and for a terrible moment he thought he would pass out. Then a pair of hands grabbed him under the arms and lifted him up. Slocum and the stranger each took hold of Curly and dragged him through a hell of falling shells to shelter under a rocky overhang.

Curly's wound wasn't serious, but without help he wouldn't have made it. The man who had helped them introduced himself as Joe Didion. He bandaged Slocum's bleeding forehead with a torn piece of shirt, and the three of them waited for the cannon fire to stop. There would be others for them to go back and help.

The cannon fire stopped at dawn.

The silence was sudden and eerie. It brought with it a strange chill. They stood and looked out into the thin, morning light. Nothing through the long night they had just survived—not the noise of cannon, not the agonized shrieks—had prepared them for what they saw before them. They stood there, too shocked to speak.

Curly was the first to find his voice. "There ain't no bodies," he choked. "They all been blowed to hell."

"No reason for it." Joe Didion slowly sat down. He was a large-boned, strongly built man, but he looked as if his strength were melting from him. He pushed out with a thickly callused hand as if he hoped to push the scene from his vision. "I hate both your sides."

"You helped us," said Curly.

"Two days ago, I had a farm near here." Didion's voice was flat and numb. "One of your armies destroyed it. Killed my woman. I picked up my gun and started shooting. Didn't care who I shot. Fell in with you men last night by accident. Just an accident."

Slocum's forehead throbbed and burned. He stared with disbelief. Over four hundred men. Blown into bits and fragments. "Marsden's Treachery."

"What's that, Major?" asked Curly.

"The name for this hellhole. Marsden's Treachery."

"Marsden lit out back for Montgomery," Curly said. "You know that, Major."

"He doubled back and betrayed us to the Yankees."

"For what purpose," Didion said. "You rebs were a beaten bunch."

"No military purpose." Slocum's wound leaked a hot

streak of blood. "But only someone who knew our line of retreat could have set up this ambush."

Curly protested, "It makes no sense, Major."

"Marsden couldn't have things his own way. So he betrayed us."

"Insanity," said Didion. "All of it's insanity. God help us all."

"Marsden will survive this war," said Slocum. His head felt on fire. "His kind don't get caught in battle. If I live, some day, somewhere, I'll kill him. With the help of God, or with the Devil, I will kill Marsden."

4

Ora Grande was the kind of place where it took no imagination to live. A one street town. A church at one end and a school at the other. The bank stood in the center of town, across from the stage station, and the sheriff's office was down a ways from the station. There were the usual small town businesses and they all prospered.

Slocum eased the wagon down the street. Fortunately, they could enter and leave without passing the sheriff's office. Curly was clucking his tongue, his eyes darting rapidly from left to right. Dorsey was whistling an unrecognizable tune. He doffed his hat and smiled to a pair of pretty ladies. There were very few people on the street. They passed a white-aproned storekeeper sweeping his wooden sidewalk. Outside of the barber shop, the barber sat on a chair waiting for a customer. He waved a friendly greeting and Slocum nodded in return.

Slocum halted the wagon in front of the bank. Curly and Dorsey dismounted with casual ease and tied their horses to the hitching post. Slocum glanced up and down the street. No sign of Didion. He nodded to Dorsey, who then went into the bank. As he climbed

28

down from the wagon he mentioned to Curly, "Remember to keep your hat on."

It was a two teller bank. Neither teller was busy. They glanced at the guard uniforms on Slocum and Curly and paid them no more mind. Dorsey stayed up front, keeping an eye on the tellers and the street.

Slocum pushed through a waist-high wooden gate that worked on a tight spring. It swung back and cracked Curly on a knee. They walked by an elderly lady working at a desk. She looked up at them curiously.

"Afternoon, ma'am," Slocum nodded.

"You're new," she said.

"Yes, ma'am," said Curly.

Slocum rapped on a door marked Manager. A moment later a voice said, "Come in." Slocum opened the door and went in, with Curly stepping in quickly behind him.

The office was like every bank office. There was the odor of stale cigar smoke. The walls had portraits of President Grant and George Washington, framed testimonial letters to the banker and a large map of the surrounding country. The banker sat beneath the map. He was a pale man, his shoulders rounded from years of hunching òver ledgers and reading the figures of other people's money. He glanced at the authorization Slocum handed him, then looked suspiciously at Slocum and Curly. "Where's Nelson and the others?" His voice was testy and demanding.

"Nelson's dead," answered Slocum. "One of the others is wounded."

The banker pushed back from his desk in alarm. He wasn't wearing a gun belt but his eyes moved tellingly toward a drawer.

"Relax, mister," Slocum said. "We're not outlaws. We didn't shoot them." Experience had taught Slocum that men like this were more apt to believe an outrageous story than a simple lie. "Goddamn miners tried to pull a strike the other night. We stopped them, but poor Nelson got killed."

29

"Why didn't someone ride in and tell us?" The banker was indignant. "Why wasn't Joe Didion called out?"

Slocum smiled. "The company preferred to handle it themselves." He patted his holster.

"I understand." The banker's shoulders shook with a mirthless laugh. "Joe Didion has been getting too soft lately. He'd likely slap their muscle-bound wrists and ride back home. Miners! Ignorant drunken louts. Hope you taught them a lesson."

"Shot a half dozen," Slocum said. "Hung the three leaders. Horse whipped a few more."

"Everything back in order?"

"They blew up a shaft. Put the work back a whole week."

"Such destruction." The banker pursed his lips and shook his head.

Slocum decided it was time to get to business. "Things are still tense out there. We'd like to load up and hurry on back."

Concern crossed the banker's face. "Didn't lose too many of you guards?"

Slocum lowered his eyes to the floor. "Just poor Nelson."

"Pity." The banker took a large, ornately engraved watch from his vest pocket. He looked closely at Curly. "Do I know you?"

Curly cleared his throat. "Been to town once or twice. You maybe seen me."

"You look familiar." He tapped the watch with a manicured fingernail and studied Curly for a moment. The watch chimed a melody when he opened its casing. "I'm afraid it will be another hour or so before I can turn over the payroll."

"We don't got no time for waitin'," Curly snapped.

Slocum shot a hard glance to Curly.

"You're going to have to wait." The banker tapped his watch. "Our money shipment was delayed. Wells Fargo threw a wheel and broke an axle outside of town.

They rode in and got a new axle from the station." The watch chimed again when he opened it. "Shouldn't be more than an hour."

Slocum took Curly aside and quietly said, "We'll have to nerve this through. You keep the scum sucker busy. Don't let him get suspicious. I'll alert Dorsey."

He found Dorsey flirting with a young woman who was making a deposit. He went to the window and looked out. Immediately, he leaped back. Joe Didion was standing across the street talking with someone.

Dorsey came up behind Slocum. "Didion don't look so tough. Looks a little fat."

Slocum explained the situation.

The kid showed no alarm at the news. "An hour, huh?" He glanced at the woman he'd been flirting with and smiled. "A man can do a lot in an hour."

"We'll be fine if we don't lose our nerve, kid."

"Just wondering if I shouldn't amble down to the saloon and buy some courage for Curly." Dorsey stood looking out the window, head cocked, arms crossed. "Regular beer belly on your old friend out there. Lawman must have a soft life. Real soft. Hard to believe he was all I heard he was. True he faced down Doc Holliday?"

"Nope. The Doc's still alive."

"What kind of shit weapon is that he wears?"

"He calls it his town tamer. It's a cut-down Winchester."

"Short barrel 'chester. Can't be too accurate."

"Better than a hand gun. He mainly uses it to crack skulls. With a hand gun Joe never had trouble dropping a man a hundred yards distant."

"I plain don't believe that, Slocum. But since I got an hour to kill, I'll do it chatting to the pretty ladies." Dorsey started away from the window. Over his shoulder he said, "Unless maybe you want me to run out for coffee and sandwiches."

Slocum removed his hat and peeked an eye out the window. Joe was still there. Damn! He hoped Joe

31

would leave before Wells Fargo pulled in. He hoped to Christ Joe wouldn't decide to help transfer the money shipment.

You have put on weight, thought Slocum as he looked at his old friend, *but I know damn well you haven't gotten soft. You've put on weight and you've come a long ways and we've saved each other's life too many times for one of us to kill the other today. You, me and Curly. We got through the war together, rode together off and on until you managed to pull yourself off the outlaw trail.*

Slocum breathed a sigh of relief as he saw Joe turn and amble down the street. He remembered his last meeting with Joe. It had been a few years ago. Slocum had been sitting in a saloon in a Texas cattletown. He was sitting at a window casing the activity in the shipping office across the street when Joe had pushed through the saloon's swinging doors. Joe was wearing a strange side arm.

"Howdy, John."

"Joe." Slocum nodded. He went to the bar and got a glass from the bartender and returned and poured Joe a shot from his bottle. "Been a while, Joe. Things good?"

"Yep. You'll have to drink that yourself. I only take an occasional beer these days."

"What brought that about?"

"A pretty good cause." Joe smiled broadly. "Got married. I've got a baby, too."

"Glad to hear it." Slocum raised his drink in toast and drank it. "What's that you're carrying?"

Joe told him what he called the weapon. "Double width stock is special made. The barrel's cut to eleven inches. It's reinforced to take heavy charge ammunition. I don't have to shoot it very often."

"Why the name town tamer?"

"I'm no longer an outlaw. I hire myself out to clean up towns. I do what I'm paid to do. I'm not a bounty hunter. If I take a man with a bounty on his head, I

32

collect it. There are a lot of towns and I have steady employment. I hope to find one where I'll be appointed or elected an official lawman. A quiet little place where I can raise my family and have time to read a few books."

"You working now?" Slocum asked with a grin.

Joe nodded. "Funny the way things happen. I fell in with you and Curly Boyle the night of Marsden's Treachery. I put on a gray uniform because you made one available to me. Fought like a bastard the whole damn war because I think I secretly wanted to get killed. After the war I come west and get on the outlaw trail for the same reason. You and Curly went back to your original homes because you wanted peace, but the circumstances forced you both out here. Damned if the three of us don't end up riding now and again together. Only now I'm the one to ride the straight line and you and Curly, well I've seen enough wanted posters on the two of you to paper a house. Sure hope you're only passing through this town, John."

"Only passing, Joe." Slocum had smiled, and he had raised and swallowed back the drink he'd poured for Joe.

"John!"

Curly's shout was like an alarm clanging through the bank. It came from the office, but the still closed door did little to muffle the panic in the shout. Three customers at the tellers' windows looked up. The tellers and the elderly lady at her desk turned, startled, as Dorsey bolted toward the office. Slocum glanced quickly out the window—Didion was nowhere in sight—and ran behind Dorsey.

The elderly lady was on her feet. Dorsey roughly spun her out of his way and charged on into the office, slamming the door behind him. The woman fell against Slocum. He caught and held her up and had to waste seconds trying to ease her concern with calming words. She wasn't listening. Her frail shoulders fought against his hands. The others in the bank were watching them.

Slocum counted on his guard uniform to command authority. He gestured for one of the tellers while saying, "Calm her. Nothing's wrong."

"That shout—?"

Slocum would never know where he found the explanation. "My friend's an epileptic."

"We'll send for a doc—" the teller started to say.

"I carry medicine with me," Slocum called back as he went through the office door.

The banker, his face white, was shaking with pain and fear behind his desk. He was cradling a broken, bloody hand in the crook of his opposite arm. He moaned, but the pressure of Dorsey's gun against his ear kept him from crying out his hurt. Dorsey was looking mean and angry. A quick glance around told Slocum there was reason for the anger.

Curly's gun was shaking in his hand. His hat lay on the banker's desk, next to the banker's ornate watch.

"Holster your gun," said Slocum. "Before you fire it by accident."

"Weren't my fault! John."

"Put it away and lower your voice." As Curly holstered his gun, Slocum drew his own. It looked like everything was about to blow. He wanted to be ready.

"He lost his nerve," Dorsey said. "We can't sit here waitin' for no payroll."

"I was keepin' him busy like you said to, John. Started talkin' to him 'bout his watch," babbled Curly. "Nice watch. You got to admit that. I started to examine it. Took off my hat. Accidental. Didn't mean to. He rec'nized my bald head. Went for a gun an' I had to kick the drawer shut on his hand. What would you of—?"

Slocum silenced the babble with a slap. The blow sent Curly reeling back against a wall. Slocum picked up the watch.

"John Slocum." The banker spoke through clenched teeth. "Now I recognize you. Joe Didion's got wanted

34

posters on the both of you. He's mentioned riding with you."

"He didn't set this up, mister." Slocum tightly gripped the watch. *"Damn."* He glanced at Curly.

"Don't hit me 'gain," Curly blubbered.

"Get yourself under control, or I'll knock you out and leave you for Didion."

Dorsey's gun was still pinning the banker to his desk. He said, "I'm listening to you, Slocum."

"It's all short hairs, kid. People out there think we got an epileptic here. You go out and tell them everything's fine. Our banker friend here will shove his hand into a pocket and take me to the vault. We'll bag up what cash is here. When I come out of the vault, I'll nod and we'll take everybody and lock them in the vault. Then we mount up and ride out."

"You can't," the banker said. "We'll suffocate. I'm the only one who knows the combination."

"Joe Didion will know how to blow you open," said Slocum.

"How about hostages?" Dorsey asked.

Slocum shook his head. "Just slow us down and make us noticed."

"What about the wagon?" said Dorsey. "Too heavy for any speed."

"That's Curly's problem. He's driving it."

"John!" Curly's voice squeaked with fear. "I won't have a chance."

"Only one you got." Slocum held out the watch. "You'll have time to think about this."

There was a knock on the door, and then the voice of the old lady calling for the banker. Slocum moved toward the door, while Dorsey scraped the sight of his gun down the banker's cheek. "Answer her nicely," Dorsey told the banker, but before the man could answer the woman called again.

"Okay," the banker gasped. "Everything is okay."

But the old lady wasn't listening. The door burst

open and she stuck her head in. With a quick, unthinking movement Slocum thrust the watch into a pocket, grabbed the woman and pulled her into the office. She started screaming before he got a hand over her mouth.

Dorsey leaped through the door. "Hands up! All of you," he shouted to those in the bank.

"Curly, help him get those people back here." The old lady was struggling against Slocum, showing more courage than Curly. "Latch the front door. Draw the shades and blinds."

"Sure, John." Curly's head nervously bobbed up and down. "I'm okay now, John."

"Then move, dammit!"

Curly skooted into the bank. The old lady continued to fight Slocum. He worked to control her, trying all the while to keep his gun on the banker. Suddenly, she bit down on his hand. "Jesus Christ!" He released her and as she fell forward, he spun her around and gave her a back-handed clip under the jaw. He caught her as she fell and eased her unconscious body to the floor.

"Sadistic bastard," the banker yelled as he started to rise from his desk.

The cold black look in Slocum's eyes stopped the banker and turned his complexion an even paler shade. "I hate hitting old ladies," Slocum said grimly. "I don't at all mind killing bankers. Let's move to the vault."

The tellers and customers were lined up facing the wall. Dorsey was talking easily to them, letting them know who was in charge but not being overly frightening about it. Curly had latched the door and drawn the shades; he was now at the tellers' windows scooping cash into a bag.

The vault was in the rear of the bank. The banker sobbed over his broken hand as Slocum pushed him to the vault.

"Ti—time lock. Can only be opened cer—certain times of day."

Slocum pushed the barrel of his gun into the banker's back. "It opens in sixty seconds."

The banker dropped to his knees and went to work on the combination.

Curly finished cleaning out the tellers. "Maybe two and a half, John. No more." He began going through the pockets of the men facing the wall, dropping their wallets into his bag.

The banker finished with the combination. He got to his feet, took hold of the handle and pulled open the heavy vault door. Slocum pushed the man ahead and the two of them entered the vault. Slocum grabbed two money sacks from a shelf and threw them to the banker. "Fill 'em. No coins!"

The vault was small. Too small. Slocum realized that if they squeezed everybody in here, there wouldn't be air enough to last them more than an hour. They would just throw the men in. He'd take their belts and suspenders and tie and gag the women. Shouldn't take more than a couple of minutes. The problem was time. Any moment now someone out on the street was bound to notice the bank being locked and the shades pulled. Most people probably wouldn't think much about it. Didion would.

The banker finished filling the sacks. "Approx—proximately thirty-two thousand."

Slocum whistled for Dorsey's attention and tossed the first bag to him. He took the second sack from the trembling banker. "I know your kind, mister. You've more money around here. You're scared lily-white but you'd rather die than lose it. I don't have time to sweat you." He raised a leg and booted the banker's chest. The man fell to the back of the vault.

Slocum moved out of the vault. "You men. Remove your belts and suspenders. Quick. Then move your asses back here."

Suddenly Dorsey dropped to one knee, aimed his gun toward Slocum and fired. The bullet whizzed past Slocum's ear. Slocum was within a hair of shooting back when he heard the banker crash to the floor behind him. He turned to see the man sprawled dead across the floor of the vault, a gun still in his hand. From some-where in the vault he'd taken a gun.

The women began screaming. "He was 'bout to get you, Slocum," shouted Dorsey.

The kid had just alerted the town, but Slocum could hardly criticize him. Slocum shoved his money sack under his arm. "Let's move!"

Curly reached the door first. He didn't take time fiddling with the latch and shot the door open. He ran out, firing wildly, scattering any who might be on the street. Dorsey was close behind Curly.

Curly was spurring his mount up the street as Slocum ran low out the door. A shot rang past him and he dove to the sidewalk. Dorsey pulled loose his mount's reins, leaped into his saddle and lashed the horse into motion.

Didion was coming up the street, running a low and twisting pattern to avoid being a target. Three men cautiously followed him. His town tamer was out, belching fire and lead. He wasn't taking time to aim, but his shots were coming close. One burned near Slocum's shoulder. Dorsey's hat was taken by another as he rounded a corner, firing back over his shoulder.

Slocum was left with the wagon. If he could get to it. He was still on the sidewalk, trapped by the lead from Didion's town tamer. Dorsey's bullets had caused the three men behind Didion to hit the ground, but Didion was still coming. Slocum planted a shot at Didion's feet, and Didion leaped behind a water trough. Slocum threw a shot over the trough, then rolled off the edge of the sidewalk. He threw the money sack into the wagon and pulled himself into the wagon seat.

"Slocum! Tall sonofabitch, I recognize you!" Didion shouted as Slocum fought to get the wagon moving. "Give it up before I have to kill you."

Slocum slapped the reins and the wagon lumbered into motion. Bullets clanged against the cage in the wagon box. At least the damn thing was bulletproof. Curly was clearly out of town; trailing in Curly's cloud of dust, Dorsey had disappeared.

The horse struggled against the weight of the wagon, barely managing to maintain a trot. Slocum knew he could never escape on this thing. He opened a couple of buttons on his shirt and shoved the money sack inside, then got out his knife. If he could cut loose one of the horses, he might have a chance. He leaped onto a horse, took a firm hold on its mane, and leaned down to cut the leads.

Then, from out of nowhere, Dorsey appeared beside him. He was leading an extra horse and grinning, cocky as hell, as if there weren't bullets flying all around him.

"Found this for you, Slocum." Dorsey guided the horse to within reach of Slocum's grasp. The wagon's cage clanged with the ringing noise of bullets. "You and me haven't worked our own things out yet."

Slocum grabbed hold of the horse's reins. "Yes, we have, kid." The horse was a spirited animal and he had a hard time slowing it and maneuvering it near enough to the team horse he still rode to make the switch.

Dorsey dropped back. He shouted as he began to fire, "I'll cover you while you change horses."

The horse continued to try and lunge ahead of Slocum. When he managed to get the animal where he wanted it, he gave up his hold on the reins, threw his arms around the animal's neck and leaped into its saddle. He dropped low, reaching blindly until he again caught the reins, then spurred the horse into a full gallop.

He felt the force of the explosion against his back. Felt it before he heard it. He glanced over his shoulder. Dorsey's horse, or what was left of it, was on the ground. The air was full of dark smoke and floating bills of money.

Slocum immediately realized what had happened. There was no point in slowing down. He cleared town and continued to spur the horse. Curly was out of sight, but Slocum would likely find him where they had staked their fresh mounts. No one was following. Curly's diversionary tactic had worked. Dorsey hadn't thrown away all of his dynamite. A bullet had hit his saddlebag. The explosion had to have shocked Joe Didion's town. And before Joe could mount a posse, he would have to pull his people away from the free floating money.

They had staked out their fresh horses in a grove of pines. Slocum pulled his stolen horse to a stop as Curly emerged to greet him.

"Damn! John. Gettin' worried 'bout you. Dorsey?"

"Didn't make it." He leaped from the horse and sent it running with a slap on its ass. He threw the money sack to Curly. "Split it with what you got. We've a ten- or fifteen-minute lead before Didion gets here and I don't want to be with you."

"John, don' be that way!"

"Split the money."

"Already counted my sack. One o' them wallets I took had over a thousand in it."

"That's good news, Curly." Slocum removed the tethers from his fresh horse. "Real good news. We maybe made ten thousand apiece." He turned around and faced Curly.

"Sorry, John." Curly was pointing a gun at him. It shook in his hand. "Got no choice."

"Put that away before you shoot yourself."

"Twenty thousand jus' ain't what I had in mind, John. Maybe it'll git me started. Wouldn't do this if I didn't have to."

Slocum started toward him. "Put it down."

"Not another step, John."

"If it's still out when I get to you, I'll beat you silly with it."

"It's like I said. I just cain't take it no more." Curly began backing up. "If I don't kill you, you'll just come after me."

Slocum continued toward him. "You're shaking too much to shoot straight."

Curly braced the wrist of his gun hand with his other

hand. He fired. The bullet slammed into Slocum's chest and he was thrown backwards. His heels tripped out from under him. Then darkness swept over him as he fell.

5

"He alive enough to hang, sheriff."

"What's keepin' him that way?"

Slocum could feel hands pressing against his chest. He vaguely heard voices, but he was still lost in darkness. Painful, black darkness.

"Watch here in his vest pocket. Deflected the bullet into his lungs."

"Tall sonofabitch always was lucky." Joe Didion's voice floated from a far place. The words bounced against Slocum's ears. "How bad is he bleeding?"

"Just a trickle on the outside. I'd guess pretty bad inside. He's got a mouthful of blood."

"For God's sake, roll him over." Slocum was slowly swimming up from the deep blackness. He recognized an urgency in Joe's harsh tone, but the voice remained dull and distant. He wanted to call out and tell Joe everything was all right. Then Joe's voice reached him again. "We don't want him drowning in his own blood. And throw me up that watch."

Two men took hold of Slocum and turned him over. A blaze of white light streaked through him, and his heart became a sudden violent hammer. He clearly heard the crunch of broken ribs grinding together. The jagged end of a rib cut into his lungs and lit a charge. Only the searing heat of the pain kept him from falling back into dark unconsciousness. A scream built inside of him but was silenced by a gush of blood. His body heaved and jerked beyond his control. He was aware of something warm against his face and realized the sensation had been created by his blood.

"Startin' to come around now, sheriff."

41

"Say, sheriff, this tree here's got a limb just the right height for a hanging."

"Tie his hands behind him," Joe ordered. "Make sure he's carrying no weapons."

Men set to work following Joe's orders. They laughed the grim, obscene laughter of a mob. Every phrase or word spoken brought more laughter. Their voices became a single raucous blur, but Joe Didion's voice wasn't among them. Slocum listened for Joe as hands roughly searched him. Every touch jolted him. His arms were twisted behind him. They were bent near to the breaking point and tied. He took his breath in slow, weak gasps. Each breath felt like an inhalation of fire. Blood continued to spill up from his lungs. Gradually it slowed, then stopped. His pain was becoming its own narcotic; he was growing numb. He concentrated on listening for Joe's voice and refused to give in to the numbness.

"He's tied tight as a Christmas package, sheriff."

"Take his boots," Joe said.

"Hell, they ain't worth the takin'. Thinner 'n my wife's chest."

"You piebald idiots. That's John Slocum," Joe responded. "If he's got an ounce of strength left in him, he'll find a way to use it. Now take the goddamn boots before he starts kicking in your heads."

Hands pulled at his boots. Someone said, "Why you think his partner double-crossed him?"

"I would imagine some quite mundane reason," Joe said flatly. "Money."

"Let's hang the bastard slow. Use a slip knot 'stead of a noose."

"Nobody's doing any lynching," Joe said.

The men protested. From the blur of their voices, Slocum had no idea how many there were, nor if Joe would be able to control them. Slocum strained to see, but his vision wouldn't focus and the shouting men were a shifting, shapeless mass.

"Dammit, sheriff, he and them other two killed one of our leading citizens. Got off with our money."

"One of our leading assholes, you mean," answered Joe. "If you boys hadn't been so damn eager to gather up all those free bills floatin' around town, we would likely have caught up with this one before his partner double-crossed him."

The voices grumbled and became more threatening.

Joe shouted, "None of you ever had more than a hundred dollars in that bank. You all pulled more than that out of the air and put it in your pockets. That makes every one of you as big a thief as this one laying here on the ground."

"We know you used to ride with Slocum."

"You're protecting him!"

"String him up!"

Joe fired off a shot from his town tamer. "You want vigilante law, you vote me out next election. Or there's enough of you to take me out now. But I guarantee at least four of you won't see tomorrow."

Slocum heard the men curse and grow silent. "Now then, two of you pick him up and throw him up here across my saddle. We're taking the river route back to town. Just so none of you gets any ideas behind my back, you'll ride ahead of me."

"Why the river route?"

"It'll take us past Doc Lyon's house. If Slocum survives Lyon and the ride, we'll give him a trial and hang him fair."

A flash of light streaked through Slocum as he was flung onto Joe's horse. The posse moved out. Slocum felt Joe nudge the horse into a slow trot. The saddle horn pushed against Slocum's chest. He tried to slide away from the horn but didn't have much success.

They had gone only a short way when Slocum's lungs began to leak again. He tried to slow the bleeding by holding his head and neck high, but every movement of the horse wrenched his broken ribs. Pain wracked and

43

weakened his every nerve; splintered bone cut him. He was being pulled into the darkness. He struggled against it but lost.

"John? Can you hear me, John?" Joe's voice drifted softly into Slocum's unconsciousness. "Speak low. The posse's only a length ahead."

Slocum's body twitched as he tried to force himself awake. Then he felt water, like a welcome rain, run down his back and shoulders. But it wasn't rain. After a moment he realized that Joe had poured the contents of a canteen over him. He opened his eyes. It was night now. His vision wasn't clear, but he saw that they were riding a narrow path along a steep incline. He heard the distant rush and tumble of a river.

"If you can't speak, John, grunt. Do something to show me you can hear."

Slocum attempted to speak. It came out as a grunt.

"Only thing that saved you was a watch in your vest pocket. From what's left of it, the watch looks to be the one owned by my town's late banker. The sonofabitch was a ripe asshole. Witnesses told me you didn't kill him. Makes no difference to me, John. If anybody other than that asshole had been killed, or if anybody had been hurt by that goddamn dynamite, I'd have let you be strung up."

Slocum forced himself to speak. "Dyna—mite wasn't my idea."

"Don't waste your energy talking." The cool edge of a knife blade slid between Slocum's bound wrists. "I'm cutting the ropes now. You'll have about two mintues to flex circulation back into your hands."

Slocum's hands fell loose as the rope was cut. His arms dropped; his wrists and fingers twitched with the sudden freedom.

"Wish you hadn't come to my town, John." Joe grunted and gave an ironic chuckle. "Expect you're wishing the same thing. You're nearer death now than you ever were that night at Marsden's Treachery. I'm

44

giving you a chance. You'll likely not make it. If God spares you, don't get within gunsight of me again."

Joe lifted Slocum and eased a belt beneath and around his chest, then pulled the belt tight and buckled it.

"Had to cut a new notch so it would fit you. I've put on a little weight. Perhaps you noticed. I like my weight and I like my town. Maybe, only maybe, the belt will hold you together some."

The belt created a band of hard pressure that localized Slocum's pain and made his breathing more difficult.

"The moon's about to skirt under a cloud. When it does, I'm going to buck my horse and throw you off. You've got about a forty-yard roll down rocks and stone. The river's high with the spring thaw. It's running fast. If you don't drown or bleed to death, you'll end up three or four miles from here. Trappers are working that area. Maybe somebody will find you and take you in."

Slocum thought about the slimness of his chances. He started to speak.

"Don't bother thanking me, John. I just don't want to see you hang. Don't want to hear your neck snap under the noose. Don't want to see your shit and piss filling your pants as you breathe your last breath, or have to smell the stink of you."

The night grew darker as a bank of clouds covered the moon.

"Good luck, John." Slocum felt Joe grab a strong hold under one of his arms. "Don't expect to see you again."

Joe bucked his horse. The animal reared high on its hind legs. Slocum was lifted like a weightless thing and thrown into space.

While still in the air, he twisted so that his hands and feet would touch ground first. There was a long, floating moment of blind suspension, then he hit. Skin

45

burned from his hands, and the breath was knocked out of him. He brought his hands up to shield his face, his bent arms covering his broken chest, and he rolled down the slope, spinning with increasing speed. He heard the shouts of the posse behind him. There were wild, scattered shots, but no bullets came near him.

Suddenly he crashed to a halt against a tree. He gripped his fingers into twists of bark and attempted to pull himself up, but dizziness and pain overcame him and he fell back to his knees. He remained crouched on his knees, gasping, until he had regained his breath.

The moon was out again, though its light didn't penetrate the shadows where he crouched. He could still hear the shouts of the posse from the top of the slope. Some of the posse continued to fire their guns, their bullets sparking the night.

His chest throbbed, his body was laced with cuts, but his lungs weren't bleeding, and the belt Joe had bound him with still held. He yearned for the luxury of resting ten minutes, but knew that any second now the men in the posse would probably come down the slope for him.

The river was only a few yards away. He crawled to it on his hands and knees. It was running fast. The water broke with white splashes against high rocks and was filled with floating debris. He dropped into it.

The shock of the cold water jolted him. The current took him and swept him under. He struggled against the force of the rushing water, but the current held him under. He bounced and tossed along the rough bed of the river. His chest started to pound with the need for oxygen. He fought his way to the surface. As he broke through, a log raced by, narrowly missing his head. He began gasping for air.

It was useless to attempt swimming. Numb with cold, he used his fading strength to stay on the surface. The white water battered and dashed him against rocks. He hit one rock with such force that he was turned around. Slocum could see a huge limb coming upon him. He swallowed air and went under. As the limb passed above, he reached and caught hold of it. He surfaced and kept his hold on the limb, wrapping his arms around it. The limb carried him down the river.

6

"Yes! God yes! Give me more."

The woman put her fingers into her mouth and bit down to stop herself from crying louder. Slocum leaned back against the edge of the bathtub and watched with pleasure as the woman squirmed on the deep length of his cock. Her breasts bobbed sensuously above the foaming surface of the bath. Circlets of white suds crowned her rosy nipples. Her wet hair whipped the air as she writhed to that unique agony of approaching climax.

He cupped her breast in his hand and lightly began squeezing and kneading it. The nipple grew hard under his molding touch. His other hand swam through their bath water and touched her where they joined. He traced through her triangle of hairs and slid a finger into her feminine cleft. She gasped at the touch of his finger against her. He kept his finger moving, stroking, as he took her breast into his mouth and sucked. She began to heave and buck wildly. His own climax was almost upon him when he wrapped his arms around her and held her. Her back arched and grew suddenly stiff. Her cunt clamped his cock. Slocum's groans joined hers as he went with his pulsing, thrusting release.

Slocum continued to hold her for the length of time it took them to regain their breaths. His cock grew soft and slipped out of her. They moved apart and each leaned back against the curving edge of the round wooden tub, their legs still twisted together in the tub's small size.

"You sure know how to fuck, mister." Her voice

was husky with satisfaction. Her features were soft and relaxed. "You sure do know how."

Slocum sighed with contentment. "You told me you only wanted to scrub my back."

She scooped up a handful of soap bubbles. "Us Frisco women are notorious fibbers." She blew on the bubbles, sending several floating through the air.

It was Slocum's fifth day in San Francisco. He'd used the first three days playing poker to get himself a stake and had met the woman yesterday in a waterfront saloon. He had just ended a grueling, but profitable, fifteen-hour session with some Russian seamen who spoke little English and played cards as well as they spoke the language. He had been headed for bed, though it was high noon, and had wanted only a night-cap until the woman had smiled at him.

He hadn't been with a woman for a long time. The Russians had provided him with money enough to do what he had come to San Francisco to do—gain entry into the Palace of Pleasure and begin his search for Curly Boyle. He decided he was entitled to a few hours of play.

He had still been wearing the hand-me-downs given him by the trappers who'd rescued and taken him in a few months back. His hair hung nearly to his shoulders and a walrus-size mustache drooped over his mouth, but the woman's smile told him she wasn't put off by his somewhat grubby appearance.

That was yesterday. They had come to his hotel and now, for twenty-four hours, they had been at it. They had talked little—conversation was hardly their mutual interest—but he had learned that her husband was a seaman some three months gone and due back next year. She wasn't a prostitute. She would put up with her husband's absence until her needs sent her out for a man.

Slocum helped the woman step from the tub. He threw her a towel and said, "Since you didn't wash my

48

back, dry it. Then we'll go get something to eat. I seem to have worked up an appetite."

"Strange," she smiled. "You've certainly done plenty of eating."

He took her to lunch and thought that would be the end of it. But she followed along while he went to the tailor shop to pick up the suit he'd ordered. She then accompanied him as he went about buying the items he needed, approving of the pair of boots he chose, watching him select a Colt .44 in a gunsmith's shop, and covering her ears while he test fired the gun in the smith's backyard range. She was impressed by the accuracy of his shooting.

He offered to buy her something. A dress, a piece of jewelry.

She refused. "I've gotten what I want from you, mister."

She got more. They returned to the hotel for another session. Then it was time for Slocum to get back to his reason for coming to San Francisco. The woman lay on the bed and watched while he took out his new suit and began to get dressed.

"You're going up the hill, aren't you?" she asked.

"This town is full of hills," Slocum answered.

"Madame Lu's. You didn't buy that fancy suit for me. You're going to her house on the hill."

"Yes," he said. "I am."

The dealer had silver hair and a smile that promised money. An ivory-colored Chinese character was printed on the blue backs of the cards. The game was blackjack, but that wasn't the game the dealer was dealing.

Slocum cupped his hands over the two cards he'd been dealt and thumbed up the edges for a look-see. A seven and a four. He kept his lean features as rock steady as he would have, had the game been honest. There were three other players plus the dealer at the table. The dealer was showing a nine over his hole card. Slocum wasn't quite sure from where the nine

49

had come, but he damn well knew it hadn't come from the top of the deck.

He had entered the game three hours ago with five one-hundred-dollar white chips and now had a pile of nineteen chips. Near his chips stood a stemmed, cut-glass goblet containing a large shot of Tennessee sour mash and a hammered metal ashtray with a Cuban cigar. The cigar had been given to Slocum by the player on his right, a man called Commissioner. The sour mash was on the house.

Slocum tapped an inch of white ash from his cigar into an ashtray and brought the smoke to his mouth. A Chinese character was part of the ashtray's hammered design, the same character that was on the cards.

"See that heathen squiggle, stranger?" The Commissioner tapped an arthritic finger against the ashtray. His round face was framed by a thick set of gray muttonchops. "It's a Chinese word. Means hope." He laughed. His thick nose was streaked with broken veins. His cheerful laughter brought a red tint to the nose. "Right about now the madame's no doubt hopin' your luck'll change."

Slocum wondered how much longer he was going to win. In a crooked game it was just plain good sense to make someone other than the dealer appear to be winning. What Slocum hadn't yet figured out was why he'd been picked to play the shill. Not that the house was losing any money. The fat player on his left had dropped well over twice the amount Slocum had been allowed to win.

Slocum eased back in his chair and puffed his cigar. His eyes rose with the drift of the pale smoke and cut through a haze of smoking tobacco and sweet-scented incense fumes. Flickering light from high, oil-burning chandeliers gave the haze a dusty, amber appearance. He glanced to the left, to the long bank of chuck-a-luck tables, then to the row of roulette wheels standing off to the right. Damn near every known game of chance was available here. Slocum hadn't yet seen a cockfight—but he wouldn't have been surprised to learn that somewhere on the premises one was in progress.

It was a crowded and curious place. Green velvet draperies covered the walls. Gigantic multicolored kites shaped like butterflies, dragons and birds hung from the ceiling. Six-foot-high white ionic columns stood throughout the room. On top of each column, incense fumed from the nostrils of a stone lion. The high, curved, copper ceiling was sculpted with winged cherubim and angels blowing shell-shaped horns, and a huge stone Buddha squatted near the main entrance. Negro attendants, dressed in a livery that predated the Revolution, serviced every table.

"Card, Mr. Hellman?"

The dealer's voice brought Slocum's attention back to the table. The dealer was speaking to the first player, a tense pinch-faced man dressed all in black except for a starched white collar cutting into his chin. He looked like a deacon, a very rich deacon, who had slipped out for a secret night.

"Good Christ, Hellman." The fat player sitting between Slocum and Hellman snorted with contempt. "Make a goddamn decision so the rest of us can play."

The Commissioner chuckled. "The way you play, Garth, would make hair grow on a wooden leg."

"Don't you ride me, Commissioner," the fat man growled. "I don't want no rides from you tonight."

"Hell, Garth, you know I take my rides upstairs." The Commissioner turned to Slocum. "Been upstairs, stranger? Been to the third floor yet?"

"Not yet," Slocum answered.

Slocum shifted in his chair and moved his long legs into a more comfortable position. His new broadcloth suit still felt strange, and he wasn't entirely relaxed in his dandy's shirt with its white ruffles. A barber had cut, parted and greased his hair into a city style that seemed to pull at his scalp. The mustache he'd grown over the past months had been trimmed, waxed and

51

curled. Still, the disguise provided by city clothes, city hair and a fancy-dan mustache more than made up for the mild discomfort. Not even an old friend was likely to recognize him.

The Commissioner said, "Upstairs, stranger, just might be the end o' your natural life." He raised a stein of beer and drank deeply. Flecks of white foam dotted his muttonchops when he put down the stein. He grinned. "Down here we gamble, up there we gambol. Get it?"

"Hellman," the fat man growled, "you playing?"

"Now, Garth, Hellman's waiting the word from God. Or maybe from one o' them tin angels on the ceiling."

A high-pitched voice behind Slocum said, "Mr. Commissioner, you speak ill of us. You know our ceilings are of copper."

The strange voice alerted Slocum. As he looked up and behind to see who had spoken, his legs tightened and he was prepared to push back from the table and draw his gun in one swift motion.

The voice belonged to a short, reed-thin Chinaman. He couldn't have weighed a hundred pounds. He wasn't wearing a gun.

The Chinaman bowed slightly toward Slocum. "You are new to us."

He wore soft brocade sandals, which explained how he had been able to come up behind Slocum without Slocum being aware of him. The toes of his sandals curled into points and glittered with gold and silver threads. His silk trousers reminded Slocum of a fancy woman's pajama bottoms, and he wore a loose, large sleeved smock that fell to his hips. His thin lips were lightly rouged. There was something odd about his eyes, but what was most unusual about his appearance was his long pigtail: woven into it were numerous tiny sparkling gems. It dangled over his shoulder, on down across his folded arms, and was tied at the end with a gold bow.

"My name is Moy," he said. "I welcome you."

52

"Moy's the high mucky muck, stranger," the Commissioner said. "Anything you want, ask for Moy. Watercress sandwiches, two girls and a Shetland pony, whatever you want."

A cheerless smile crossed the Chinaman's lean features. "Should the gentleman tire of blackjack, other pleasures are available."

"I'll tell you what would pleasure me, Moy," Slocum replied softly. He stared into the Chinaman's waxy eyes. "You not creeping up behind me like a goddamn cat."

Moy's eyes, dark with fury, met Slocum's stare. A colorless tongue slid out and licked between the pink rouged lips. His head moved slowly back and forth, but his gaze remained steady. The gems in his pigtail shimmered, the long black braid undulating like the body of a snake.

All the table's attention was on them. Slocum heard the wheezing sound of Hellman's breathing and the dealer's nails tapping the deck.

Slocum realized the Chinaman could have a knife or gun hidden in one of his flared sleeves. He cursed himself for not thinking about that possibility earlier. His seated position was awkward. Should Moy go for a sleeve weapon, Slocum knew he wouldn't have time to draw his own gun. Still, if Moy made the least move, Slocum was ready to charge from his chair. The combination of speed, surprise and his greater weight would surely topple Moy off his feet. Before Moy knew what was happening, Slocum would have a gun aimed straight at him.

The Commissioner spoke. "Now, Moy, quit puttin' one of your Oriental hexes on the stranger."

A moment passed. Then Moy, as if he'd just been part of a hilarious joke, threw back his head and laughed a shrill and girlish giggle. Slocum continued to watch for a movement in the man's sleeves. The others at the table, one by one, joined Moy's giggle with forced chuckles and laughter.

"The stranger, here, he ain't used to our city ways," said the Commissioner.

The giggling stopped. The waxy glaze returned to Moy's eyes, and his cheerless smile again appeared. He bowed quite low, nearly touching Slocum. "And I, I confess, am not entirely accustomed to the ways of Western culture. It is not my nature to disturb our players by announcing my approach. To walk with the silent grace of a cat was a most unintentional error."

"I like to know what's behind me," Slocum said.

"A very American attitude. We of the East prefer to know what is ahead of us. Your name, sir?"

"Green," answered Slocum.

"Ah, Mr. Green. A most common American name."

"I come from a large family."

Moy added an unctuous curl to his smile. He bowed once again and walked away from the table.

The Commissioner sighed. "Oughtn't to've called him a goddamn cat. Damn heathen takes offense at everything."

"Who is he?" asked Slocum.

"A formidable opponent, stranger. Formidable." The Commissioner's arthritic hands took a fresh cigar from his vest pocket. He bit off the end and spat it toward a spittoon. "He's Madame Lu's cousin. Meanest sonofabitch this side of the Mississip'."

The fat man slapped the table. "Let's play cards."

"Notice that sweetish smell on his clothes?" the Commissioner asked Slocum. "Smelled like scorched molasses? Opium. Moy has hisself a pipe every hour or so. Some say he's more mellow when he's piped to the eyeballs like he was now. Others think a pipe just makes him meaner. If I was you, stranger, I'd stand well away from him. Stay out o' reach of his pigtail. It ain't just a fairy's braid. He can swing it like a 'gator snaps its tail, whip it into a man's face. All them shiny stones got sharp edges. Cuttin' edges.

54

An' then . . . well, let's jus' say Moy's got other tricks up his sleeve."

"Mr. Green," the dealer said to Slocum, "don't listen to everything the Commissioner says. Moy is the reason the Palace of Pleasure has very little trouble and highly satisfied customers."

Slocum was using the name Green because it was an alias unknown to Curly Boyle. The Palace of Pleasure was Slocum's only lead on Curly. The lead was three months old. It was likely Curly was no longer in San Francisco. He was prepared to track Curly to the ends of the earth if necessary. And one thing was sure—the tracking would be a damn sight easier if Curly didn't know Slocum was after him.

When the hand finally came to an end, the dealer was showing twenty. He said, "House pays twenty-one, gentlemen."

Slocum showed his hand and collected another white chip. The Commissioner and Hellman pushed away their cards without showing them. Hellman meekly announced he was quitting and left the table.

The Commissioner winked at Slocum. "Hellman always loses a few hundred before gettin' up the nerve to go upstairs. Eases his conscience to lose 'fore he has his ashes hauled."

"Commissioner," Slocum said, "you seem familiar with just about everything here."

"Uh huh." The Commissioner stroked his mutton-chops. He glanced warily at Slocum. "You wouldn't be lookin' for something, or maybe somebody, in particular, would you?"

"Truth is," Slocum said, "I'm curious to see the famous Madame Lu."

The dealer called for bets. Then he said, "Mr. Green, I've been working here a year and I've yet to lay eyes on the lady."

"She don't have to be seen," added the Commissioner. "She's got more power than any man in this state. She wants something, Moy sees to it she gets it."

"Too much power for a yellow-skinned whore." The fat man jabbed the air with a stubby finger. "It isn't going to last much longer. Thanks to the continental railroad, this city's growing as fast and as big as Chicago. There's no room left for the likes of Madame Lu."

Slocum glanced at his new cards. He was fifteen hundred dollars ahead and expected to start losing. He had been dealt an ace and a queen. "Blackjack."

"House pays double," smiled the dealer.

The Commissioner nodded toward Slocum's chips. "Won yourself enough to have a hell of a time upstairs. Might as well spend it there as lose it down here. It's the expected thing to do."

It dawned on Slocum why he'd been picked to play shill. Despite the lavish gambling parlor, gambling was hardly what had made the Palace a legend. It was logical enough for the house to think a stranger would stop only temporarily at the tables.

"Your winnings, stranger, will give you full entrance to the third floor. Don't even pause on the second."

"Why?" Slocum asked.

"Second floor's just a reg'lar cathouse. Choose your lady an' go to an open room. Oh, it's all very elegant. The girls are clean. They give you a short arm an' a sponge bath 'fore goin' into action. But it's still plain old cathouse doin's."

"Sounds fine to me." Slocum drank his remaining sour mash.

"Ah, but the third floor. Good Christ, it's damn near impossible to describe." The Commissioner's broken-veined nose became as red and large as a crab apple while he spoke. "A place of dreams. Women in all sizes, colors, any combination you can think of. Nothing under seventeen, madame won't allow that, but if you like 'em younger, well they got the costumes. If you happen to be one of those men, an' you don't look like you are, who get all excited an' can't control yourself, they got a trick of splashin' you down with paregoric. Makes things last. Then there's the Ruby twins. They do somethin' with beads. They start out wearing these skimpy, flimsy outfits and then they—"

The fat man pounded the table. "That floor is for degenerate old asses who can't get it up in no normal way."

Slocum had had enough of the tables. As he stood, the Commissioner advised, "Ask for the Ruby twins. Tell 'em you want the special."

Slocum found his way to the dining room. A couple of pounds of rare sirloin was more on his mind than a romp with a pair of girls. After eating, he would quietly ask around about Curly Boyle. He'd given up hope of finding Curly on the premises. The twenty thousand Curly had ridden off with after shooting him wouldn't have lasted Curly a week in the Palace. But Curly wasn't one to go unnoticed. And on a spree he was very apt to have dropped a word here or there that would give Slocum a lead on him.

The dining room was downright sedate compared to what else he had seen of the Palace. The lamps burned low. The ceiling had been dropped and was painted a plain white. There were many potted and hanging plants, and the greenery had been arranged to give every table its own space of shaded intimacy.

Slocum stood at the entrance for a minute. A place this luxurious was bound to have a maitre d', but none was in sight.

He watched the Negro waiters, some carrying small drink trays, others large platters heavily laden with covered serving dishes. Soon he got tired of waiting for a maitre d' and went to a table that suited his wants. The linen was thicker than a prison blanket.

He tapped a fingernail against a crystal wine glass. It rang like a Christmas bell.

Angry words were being spoken near him. He glanced over his shoulder and saw a Chinese man berating a waiter. The Chinaman wore Western clothing and had a pigtail, though it was much shorter than the one worn by Moy.

The Chinaman abruptly turned from the waiter and came to Slocum's table. He shook a finger. "You not sit here!"

Slocum couldn't believe it. First Moy. Now this one. Were all Chinese crazy?

"Not sit! You hear?" the Chinaman shouted.

"Who the hell are you?"

"I Hip Sing."

"Quit pointing your finger, Hip Sing, or I'll break it off and shove it up your ass."

The Chinaman's mouth dropped open. He blinked rapidly.

"And don't shout at me like a damn seagull," Slocum continued.

The waiter had followed behind the Chinaman. Slocum's remarks brought a smile to the waiter's face.

The Chinaman balled his hands into tiny fists and propped them on his hips. He spoke lower but with much indignation. "I maitre d'." He pronounced his title *may-ter dee*. "I no seat you here."

"You weren't around. It was hard work, but I managed to find my own table."

The waiter flashed another smile.

Hip Sing rocked back and forth on his heels. "You no un'nastand. Maitre d' have much to-do. I have to leave dining room. I tell nigger stop whoever come. He suppose to be head waiter. He no stop you. He dumb nigger. No do what I say. Now I seat you proper."

The waiter had lowered his eyes and was staring at the floor. It occurred to Slocum that a head waiter

58

would know a great deal about who came and went from the Palace.

"Hip Sing, if the man you're referring to is the man standing behind you, he was likely too busy to notice me. I watched him work. He's good. Now go away. I'm paying for my dinner and I'll eat it at any damn table I want."

The Chinaman was blinking rapidly. His whole body was shaking. He stuttered, "I—I—I report this!" He spun around and quickly left the room.

Slocum turned to the waiter. "Didn't mean to cause you any trouble."

"Weren't your fault, suh." The waiter spoke with a soft, familiar accent. "I thank you for your kin' words. But you may be the one in trouble, suh. Mr. Sing, he's Mr. Moy's man. You know 'bout Mr. Moy?"

Slocum smiled. "I've met the man." He broadened his smile. "Do I hear Arkansas?"

"Born and raised there 'till I was freed, suh. Learned my profession in a fine house." He smiled as broadly as Slocum. "I believe I hear a little bit of the ole South myself."

Slocum laughed. "Hell, I thought I'd lost the accent by now."

"It's faint, all right, but I hears it." The waiter straightened his shoulders. "If it's to your likin', suh, I'd be pleased to take your order."

"Think I could get something as simple as a steak? Charred on the outside, blood in the center?"

"Yes, suh. 'Bout an inch and a half thick?"

"Good." Then with a confiding note to his voice Slocum added, "Think I could get a mess of greens cooked up in pork fat?'

The waiter smiled again. "If you don't mind eatin' what the help eats."

The waiter disappeared. Slocum noticed Moy and Hip Sing standing at the entrance looking his way. Hip Sing was waving his arms up and down, his head wagging his pigtail like a puppy's tail. Moy, his hands hidden in his sleeves, nodded once or twice. After Moy left, Hip Sing walked through the dining room, apparently taking much care to avoid coming anywhere near Slocum.

The waiter returned carrying a tray with a covered serving dish and a glass containing a colorless liquid. As he set down the glass, he said, "Country vittles don't mix good with French wines."

Slocum took a sip. It cut through his stomach like acid. He gasped.

The waiter beamed with pride. "When my daddy taught me to make it he said it weren't good 'less it brought tears to the eyes." He uncovered the serving dish. A rich scent steamed into the air. "Possum stew. Just may be a chunk of last night's turtle swimmin' in it. A fine appetizer." He ladled a huge portion into a tureen.

Slocum tasted the stew and complimented it. He casually added, "I'm looking for an old friend. Heard he likes to come here. Name's Curly Boyle."

"Not sure I recognize the name, suh."

"Called Curly 'cause he's bald as a baby's ass. Had some kind of childhood disease. Same disease left him kind of runty legged. It would sure be worth it to me if I could find him."

"I will ask around, suh."

The waiter proceeded to bring a large number of dishes to the table. He also refilled the glass of liquor whenever it was empty. No more mention of Curly was made. By the end of his meal, Slocum was feeling light-headed.

"This friend you mentioned," the waiter said as he presented Slocum with the check. "If you was to find him, it wouldn't cause anything troublesome?"

"Not for you." Slocum shook his head to clear it of the lightness. "Is he here?"

The waiter brushed the tablecloth with a napkin. "Might Mr. Boyle wear a wig to cover his baldness?"

"Possible."

"Georgia Cracker accent?"

Slocum worked to keep his voice casual. "Sounds like him."

"A gentleman of his description is known to the waiters who handle the upper floors. I could arrange for you to surprise him there. If you care to wait at the bar." Slocum went to the bar and ordered a Napoleon brandy. A clock hung behind the bar. He was watching the gold pendulum swing away the seconds when out of the corner òf his eye he spotted Moy coming towards him.

"Mr. Green." Moy reeked with the scent of opium. His eyes were popped. "Your meal? Enjoyable?"

Slocum watched the Chinaman's sleeves and long pigtail. "Very enjoyable."

"Then you will want to make apologies to my maitre d'."

Slocum sipped his brandy and said nothing.

"You cause Hip Sing to lose face in front of waiter. Waiter is servant to Hip Sing. If waiter do not wish to serve Hip Sing, waiter is free to work elsewhere. If you do not wish to honor our hospitality, you too are free to go."

There was nothing to gain in continuing with the Chinaman. "Before I leave," Slocum said, "I'll speak with Hip Sing." Sure he would. Like hell he would.

"If you do not, you shall be most unwelcome in the future." Moy took a step backward and bowed. His pink lips curved an oily smile. "After all, is it not true? A happy guest is he who brings happiness to his hosts."

Slocum waited until Moy walked away before turning back around to the bar. He glanced at the clock. Not two minutes had been chewed up. He finished his brandy and waited.

The Commissioner slid in beside him. "Buy you a drink, stranger?"

Slocum accepted the drink with a nod.

61

"Heard yet what Moy keeps up his sleeves?" asked the Commissioner.

"Derringer?" guessed Slocum.

"Chinese knives. You an' me call 'em meat cleavers. One in each sleeve. He can pull 'em faster than most men can draw."

Slocum grinned with disbelief.

"Saw a fella draw on him once," the Commissioner said. "Fella wasn't the slowest I ever seen. Managed to clear his leather 'fore Moy's pigtail raked over him. Half second later the fella's gun hand was on the bar. Weren't attached to no arm. Moy's cleaver had sliced it clean off. Poor bastard later bled to death outside. Moy's just plain evil." The Commissioner's features were ruddy and full and he was more than drunk. "Take that card game we was in. Most games here are straight. Moy rigs one or two a night. Don't need the loot. He's one of those people just needs to steal."

"If you knew the game was rigged, why did you stay in it?" Slocum asked.

The Commissioner's chuckle was raucous, crackling. "Got nothin' to lose. Ain't goin' to live long enough to spend my money." He raised a crippled hand and shook the gnarled limb like it was a hard won thing. "Arthritis. Plain to see. What don't show is a liver big as tomorrow, hard as a Baptist Sunday. I creak when I walk. My heart's the size of a jackrabbit's head. Life has its woes, stranger. Let's drink to life. Let's proceed to git drunk an' tell dirty jokes."

Slocum watched the swinging pendulum.

The Commissioner ordered another beer and drank it fast. He chattered and laughed, as if his jackrabbit heart had told him tonight was to be his joyful last, and after a while he began to nod drowsily. His nose would just about touch the bar, then his head would snap up and he would chuckle and say something totally meaningless.

Finally the waiter approached and beckoned. Slocum left the Commissioner asleep at the bar and followed the waiter through a door marked private into a dark hall. It was bare and narrow. The waiter led the way with a lantern; its fumes were harsh and pungent. Shadows flickered against the walls.

Slocum pushed the skirts of his jacket behind his gun. He moved the gun up and down in its holster and kept his hand on it. As they came to a stairway, the waiter stopped and turned to Slocum. He held the lantern in one hand, and in his other hand was a key.

"A passkey, suh. Opens to a room where there's a gentleman answering the description of Mr. Boyle. It cost me to obtain it, suh."

Slocum looked at the key. The light from the lantern flickered along its brass surface as if it were on fire.

"How much?" he asked.

7

Slocum walked casually along the third floor corridor so as not to gain the attention of anyone he might come upon. A thick carpet swallowed the sound of his boot heels. Muffled noises seeped from behind closed doors. Behind one an organ played a hymn; behind another someone was neighing. He passed but one couple, a tall woman and a skinny man. The woman wore a crown of antlers and a tight, floor-length gown that accentuated her large curves. She led the man by a leash attached to a collar around his neck.

He came to the door he wanted. Behind it was what the waiter called the playroom suite. Curly, or a gentleman of his description, was somewhere in the suite. It booked at two hundred dollars an hour, and the gentleman had signed on for three hours. He had been in the suite time enough, according to the waiter, to have left the first room and gone on with his partner into the bedroom.

Slocum listened at the door but could not hear any sounds coming from the room. He glanced up and down the corridor and made sure he was unobserved, then slipped the key into the lock and pushed open the door.

No one was in the room. He went in and quickly, without a sound, closed the door.

The suite was aptly named. He was standing in a playroom, a child's playroom that was somehow lit to give the illusion of bright, yellow sunlight streaming through gauze-curtained windows. The tiled floor was littered with dolls, stuffed animals, toy soldiers, high chairs, building blocks and balls. A box of crayons spilled over crude, childish sketches of naked men and women. Cowboys and Indians chased each other around the walls. The ceiling was mirrored. A man's clothing was strewn among the toys. Also on the floor were a pair of cotton panties decorated with pink rabbits.

Soft moaning came from behind a curtained enclosure across the room. Slocum drew his gun and moved to the curtain, stepping with care to avoid hitting a toy. He used his gun barrel to part the curtain wide enough for him to see inside.

A woman with the face of a little girl was sitting on the edge of a bed. Her freckled features were framed by pink-ribboned blond curls. She wore only a peppermint-striped pinafore and a child's patent leather slippers and she was holding the hem of her pinafore to her neck to give the man who was on his knees between her legs full range of her thin body. Her eyes were closed and she was cooing and moaning childish endearments.

The kneeling man wore nothing. His face was pushed into the woman's crotch. He gurgled. He had a head of thick, black hair.

Slocum pushed through the curtain. He must have

made some sound because the woman's eyes opened and she saw him. Her pale, pouting lips parted, but the sight of Slocum's gun kept her from screaming. The kneeling man went right on with what he was doing. Slocum moved to the man, pushed his gun into the black hair and lifted away the wig.

Curly tried to pull his head from between the woman's thighs, but the pressure of the gun against the base of his skull stopped him.

"You've just eaten your last meal, Curly."

"Slocum!"

"No sudden moves, Curly."

"I'd know your voice anywhere, John."

Slocum twisted the gun barrel into the skin on Curly's bald head. "It's a .44. As I pull it back, I want you to slowly stand up from your little sister."

"Sure, John. Anything you say."

Slocum eased back. As Curly began to get to his feet, the woman pulled away and crouched at the foot of the bed. Curly's shoulder blades stuck out like little wings from his back; his skin was white as a sheet. He said to the woman, "It's John Slocum. Man I told you so much about."

The woman spoke hard and very unlike a child. "You told me he was dead."

Curly's bald head bobbed up and down. "How is it you're 'live, John?"

"Some trappers found me. Doctored me until I was well enough to earn my keep. Stayed the season with them. They gave me two hundred dollars as my share."

Curly clucked his tongue. "Well now, John, that just goes to show. You cain't get rich workin' for a livin'. Okay fer me to turn around?"

"Do it slow."

Curly turned. His skinny, hairless body looked like something the birds had already picked clean and left wanting, but his chinless jaw was crooked with

65

a cheerful grin. "Goddamn, it's good to see you, John. No hard feelings, is there?"

Slocum's fingers tightened on the trigger.

"John, you don't want to shoot. Not here."

"He's right," the woman said. "A shot would bring you more trouble than you could handle."

"Get some clothes on, Curly," said Slocum. "We're taking a walk."

Curly cocked his head. "Now, John, I think we should talk things over a—"

"Curly, in another second I start pistol-whipping you," Slocum turned to the woman. "You got clothes other than the Little Bo Peep outfit?"

She nodded to a closet. "But I ain't going no-where with you."

Keeping the gun aimed at Curly, Slocum went to the closet, opened it, found a robe and threw it to the woman. He motioned for Curly to march ahead of him into the other room. He held open the curtain and gestured for the woman to follow them.

"Get dressed, Curly," Slocum said when they were in the playroom. "Don't think about picking up your gun belt."

Curly picked up his underwear and pulled it up his skinny, bent legs. "John, you plain know you don't want to kill me."

"Hey," the woman complained. "Do I have to stay here?"

Slocum glanced at her. She was wiping away her freckles with a handkerchief. She had removed her blond curls and revealed a head of close-cropped black hair. "You wouldn't happen to have the makings on you, Slocum?" she asked.

How quick they grow up, thought Slocum. He pointed toward Curly and said, "When little brother gets dressed, he's going to tie and gag you. There ought to be some jump ropes around here."

"I didn't book for bondage," she protested.

"Ain't this Palace one whole hell of a place." Curly

was pulling on his pants. "Course, now, me an' the lady was just havin' fun. I want you to know, John, I mean to give you your full share for the bank job. My share, too. You'll have to give me a day or so to raise the cash but—"

"You know I didn't track you for money."

"Listen, Slocum," said the woman. "If you want to kill him easy, hit him over the head and throw him out of a fucking window."

"Oh, he don't want to do that," snapped Curly. "We just got a misunderstandin' to work out. Right, John? I got me somethin' mighty important to tell you."

"What would that be?" Slocum asked. Looking at the fashionable clothing Curly was putting on, he remembered the cost per hour of this suite and wondered how Curly was paying for his expensive tastes.

"Marsden," smiled Curly.

Slocum's mouth went dry. Marsden's name had reached deep and turned over his stomach. His mind tossed with the memory of the night of the Treachery. He felt tired and wanted to sit down, but a strong surge of anger flared through him. He snapped, "I might have let you off with a good beating, Curly. Not now. Not after you telling me a lie like that."

"No lie, John." Curly casually finished getting into his clothes. "Major-General Marsden. I know where he is."

"Is he here? In Frisco?"

"Now, John, before I gives you my information, we've got to make a deal. I can see where you might have it in for me. But I truly believe me for Marsden is more 'n fair."

"You expect me to take your word?"

"If I was to take you to someone who'd verify me?"

Slocum nodded. "That might do it."

Curly patted his head. "Mind if I get my hair 'fore we leave?"

"Wait." Slocum gestured to the woman. "Tie her."

"Oh, shit," the woman mumbled. She frowned but remained silent as Curly pushed her into a high chair. He tied her legs together with a pair of jump ropes and knotted them to a leg of the chair. He twisted her arms behind the chair and worked on them a short while with another jump rope. Then he gagged her with a handkerchief.

Slocum went to check the finished job. The woman's legs were secure, but when he looked behind the chair he discovered the woman's arms weren't tied. He realized Curly had held onto the last rope.

The realization came too late. He heard the whistle of the whipping rope and pulled back just as a hard wooden handle lashed open his forehead. He staggered backwards, stunned, dimly aware of Curly running into the bedroom. By the time Slocum had recovered his senses enough to follow, Curly had opened a bedroom window. An outside breeze blew the window curtains into the room, wrapping them like a web around Curly. He tore them loose as he crawled onto the sill. Slocum lunged, but Curly twisted up his runty legs and edged out along the ledge.

Slocum leaned out the window, the breeze cold against the warm gash on his forehead, and reached for Curly. His fingers caught onto a piece of torn curtain, but he couldn't quite reach Curly.

The ledge was maybe six inches wide. Curly was cautiously edging sideways along it, and the breeze was snapping his trousers. The black ground looked very far below.

"Cain't trust you, John," shouted Curly.

Slocum peered through the darkness. Where the building cornered about ten yards down the ledge, he thought he saw the pale outline of a drainpipe. Curly began to move a bit more hastily as he neared the pipe, and suddenly one of his heels slipped off the ledge. For an instant, Curly was a teetering silhouette against the night, his arms flapping like a broken-winged bird.

The stiff breeze ruffled his clothing and filled his jacket with rushing air, as he strained to get his foot back on the ledge. Somehow he did it.

"I want Marsden!" Slocum called. "Not you."

"I know you, John." Curly pressed against the wall, gasping for breath. His twisted legs shook and his hands searched the black bricks for finger holds. "You get somethin' burnin' in your mind, it don't never stop."

Curly began to move again. Slocum realized he was hoping to reach the corner and slide down the drain-pipe.

"You can't make it," Slocum cried.

"You come here for me, John, not Marsden." Curly's legs shot out from under him. He screamed.

Slocum turned away. He didn't want to watch Curly fall to his death. He waited until the body smashed against the ground before looking out the window again. Some people were running toward the body. In the darkness he could see only the lanterns they carried, like yellow flames rushing through the night. Then, from directly below, came a shout that told him what he already knew. Curly was dead.

He reached into a pocket and pulled out a bent bit of metal: the slug Curly had shot him with. He had carried it ever since the night a trapper had removed it with a pair of needle-nose pliers. He bounced the slug up and down in his palm and then tossed it out the window into the black air.

There was an odd, rustling sound behind him. It alerted him, reminding him he was a stranger in a very strange establishment. As he turned from the window, he moved his hand near his holster ready to draw. In the doorway, facing him, was an Oriental woman. She was quite lovely, and since the derringer in her hand looked quite lethal, he made no attempt to draw.

8

"John Slocum," she said, "you will come with me."

Her beauty stunned him. A blue silk kimono covered her petite body, its delicate folds parted at the neck to reveal the high, golden slope of her breasts. Her black hair, which fell in bangs across her forehead, was highlighted by a white flower behind one ear.

"Quickly, please." There was the whisper of silk on silk as she gestured with the derringer. Her voice carried an authority that outweighed her small size and relative youth. Slocum guessed she was in her mid-twenties. She looked younger, but her almond-shaped eyes had an older, wiser quality. Her eyes held him. They were amber, deep and dusky.

"No harm will come to you, John Slocum, if you do as I say. I am Han Su Lu."

He felt the surprise showing on his face.

"Yes." There was a brief flicker of amusement in her smile. "I am Madame Lu. Please come with me. You have just caused the death of a customer, an offense for which my cousin Moy would gladly give you a slow, torturous death."

"Curly fell on his own, ma'am."

"Do not toy with me, John Slocum. I saw and heard it all. Now, quickly." She gestured with her derringer, eliciting another whispery rush of silk on silk. "I assure you I shall shoot if you do not do exactly as I say."

They left the playroom suite, Slocum very conscious of her behind him. They went along the corridor and up a flight of stairs. Slocum was forced to keep himself a pace ahead. He glanced back once and saw that she walked in the Oriental fashion, hands clasped together in front of her, with the barrel of her derringer poking between her fingers like a misplaced ring. She was evidently supremely confident of her control over him. So much so that she hadn't bothered to remove his gun from his holster.

They entered a large, heavily decorated room, with fluted columns and carved cornices. There was a fire in a stone fireplace and the walls were filled with paintings. Ornate chairs, rococo settees, filigreed coffee tables spread across a Persian carpet.

"You may sit, John Slocum. Or remain on your feet." Her voice contained a melodic rhythm. "I wish for you comfort while you are in my presence."

Slocum stood in front of the fireplace. Little jade elephants decorated the hearth. He smiled and said, "Is this the Victorian suite?"

"Your wry humor suits you, John Slocum. More so than does the clothing you are wearing. I had not heard about you that you were humorous." Her smile became sly and teasing. "As it happens, we are within my chambers. Or at least, the limit of them which you shall see for this moment."

"Where did you learn your English?" he asked. "The Sorbonne?"

"The most part from stolen books. Or from sleeping with men who spoke better than I."

Her eyes continued to hold him. Her derringer still kept him from leaving, but her eyes were the magnet. They were at once chaste and erotic, darkly secretive and openly lit.

She hid her derringer in the large bow of her sash. "I believe I have your interest enough to no longer keep you at gunpoint."

"Oh, be quiet," said Slocum. "You know you have my interest. I know you brought me up here for a reason."

"Does your forehead bother you, John Slocum?"

He had all but forgotten the gash. He winced, though, as he touched it with his fingers. He went to a mirror. It looked worse than it was. The handle of the goddamn jump rope had sliced a two-inch cut.

Dried blood filled the cut and a trickle of blood had caked in an eyebrow.

"Soap and water will take care of it." he said. "How is it you know so much about me?"

"Many of your exploits have not gone unreported, John Slocum. Too, your features have been sketched unflatteringly upon wanted posters."

She crossed to a sideboard, her gown again eliciting that soft whispery sound. Slocum turned from the mirror to watch the trim, rounded slope of her ass. She opened the sideboard and took out a brandy decanter and two snifters.

She said, "I also learned much about you from the unfortunate Mr. Boyle."

Slocum laughed. "He tell you he tried to kill me?"

She crossed to him and handed him a brandy. "Actually, he told me he had killed you. Which is why he was under my employ."

Before Slocum could comment, she touched a place on the gold leaf frame of a painting and that whole section of the wall swung open.

"Come. I shall show you how I was able to arrive so quickly at the scene of Mr. Boyle's accident." Her lips slid into a provocative pout. "Do bring your brandy. You may need it."

Slocum followed her through the opened wall. He found himself on a long catwalk, running the length of an oddly lit passage about ten yards wide. The strange light streamed up through opaque glass panels, and the air was close and cloying and smelled like a sick room filled with too many flowers. Ropes, handles, levers and pullies were connected to the railing of the catwalk. "Surely you noticed, John Slocum, the nature of the business conducted on the third floor."

"Only in passing," he answered.

"Unique tastes are catered to there. While I do derive a profit by catering to such tastes, there are constant risks."

"I always heard," said Slocum, "that every business has its problems."

She halted above one of the opaque panels. "While our customers pay for privacy, it is a business precaution to discreetly check upon their conduct. I happened to pull this lever at the moment you entered the playroom suite."

She pulled a lever, and the opaque panel cleared. Slocum saw the playroom below. It was hazy, as if the panel had turned into a layer of fog, but he had no trouble seeing Little Bo Peep, again in costume, playing jacks with a new customer.

"Two-way mirrors," explained Madame Lu.

"Inscrutable," said Slocum.

She moved farther up the catwalk and stopped above another panel. "I am able to hear as well as to see. The wooden sound flues leading from below are based on ancient principle."

She pulled another lever and yanked a few handles. Beneath them, Slocum saw and heard the tense blackjack player, Hellman. The scene caused Slocum to gulp down his brandy. Hellman, naked, was crawling on his hands and knees around a pebbled surface. A woman wearing boots and spurs was riding on his back. She was spurring him and whipping his ass with a crop.

"*Aighh!*" Hellman's whine echoed through the flues. "*Ride me, ride me home.*"

Madame Lu pushed the handles and lever back into place. She opened still another panel.

The scene took Slocum's breath away. Two women were making love. No, on second look, he realized there was a third woman. The third was receiving the kisses and fondling of the other two. All three were lovely. He watched with a grim fascination. His stomach quivered, cloying fumes filled his lungs and he felt again as if he were floating. He didn't find it erotic, yet he was unable to turn away. The third woman, using both her body and voice, was urging the other two on in a manner so desperate as to be pathetic. She pulled one's large breasts to her mouth and locked the other's head between her strong, muscular legs. Her body began to violently buck and sway. A cry, more of pain than orgasm, swept the sound flues like an eerie wind. When the cry ended, the woman pushed away the others and pulled up her legs. She crouched and shivered and sobbed.

"Enough," said Slocum, aware that his throat was dry and vaguely sour.

"The bottom woman, in this instance, is our client." Madame Lu closed the panel. Her voice had altered subtly, becoming softer and breathier, like the sound of silk. "Let us return and continue our conversation."

She started back past Slocum. On the narrow cat-walk she paused, her taut breasts firmly pressed against his chest. There was the rustle of silk as one of her hands brushed his crotch. "I confess, John Slocum, to at times becoming aroused by what I chance to see."

There was challenge in her amber eyes, lit with their dark inner glow. She said, "Do such Rabelaisian scenes excite you?"

He didn't believe she was truly aroused. At least not in the way she hinted. He thought she was somehow testing him,

"I've always figured certain things," he said, "such as a Rabelaisian romp or the Inferno, are best left to the imagination."

"Men are rare in my life, John Slocum." She touched a cool hand against his cheek. "My imagination has so long been put to the services of others, that my own more common desires receive but scant release. Is that not sad?"

He followed her back down the catwalk. He touched his cheek and the cool trace that had been left by her fingers.

"Call me please, Han Su."

Slocum lay back on a settee while she cleaned his wound with a brandy-soaked cloth. When she finished, she stood back and examined her work for a few moments. She lit a slim, aromatic cigar for him and poured him another brandy. Then she left the room, returning with a basin of warm water, soap and a razor.

"You are attractive, John Slocum. However, you will be more so once I have shaved your mustache."

Slocum smiled. "I do my own shaving, Han Su."

"It is a custom of my people for a woman to serve the man. I wish to serve you."

Slocum nodded for her to go ahead. A joyful mood had come over him. The cigar was mild and smooth, the brandy warm and soothing. He lay with his eyes closed, very relaxed, while she shaved him.

She told him with drifting words that she was closing the Palace of Pleasure.

"I do so with no little unhappiness. Political pressures are being brought to bear on me. I could, of course, continue to buy off the fools and hypocrites. However, I have amassed fortune enough to achieve my life's dream, a dream so intense it has become obsession and nightmare. I have been both scarred and sustained by it. Not many have the strength to live with such dreams."

She rinsed the razor in the basin. Slocum puffed his cigar. He heard the floating drift of her voice.

"A special train is being built for me. It will be noticed wherever I travel. It will be completed within the week. We shall be traveling east, across tracks which I and my family helped construct under slave conditions. I was but fourteen during that time. We were laughed at, abused, called heathens. Those who treated us the worst were the ones most sanctimonious. Now my train shall travel the tracks laid with my people's blood. My train will accommodate forty girls and has two large club cars fitted for gambling. As we travel, we shall make frequent stops. I will profit greatly from the money brought in by my business and from knowing I have brought every sin and lust feared by those sanctimonious hypocrites into their communities."

Slocum chuckled. "A steam-driven whorehouse." He was amused by the audacity and sweet irony in her intentions. "A whorehouse on wheels." His chuckle became a high, giddy laugh.

She had finished shaving him. Slocum touched his lip. It felt full and free. Han Su stepped back and placed the shaving basin on a small table. Slocum puffed the cigar. When Han Su dropped the razor into the basin, it seemed to Slocum to make a loud and hollow sound.

"The unfortunate Mr. Boyle was to have traveled with us. I had given him the title of Protector."

"Sounds like a fancy name for pimp." He laughed and laughed. "Perfect job for Curly. Pimping for a train."

"His only duty was to protect myself. I thought the man who killed John Slocum would be capable of such duty."

"Protect you from what?"

"My cousin Moy. He does not wish to leave here. Nor is he sympathetic to my dream. I fear he may attempt to take my train, perhaps kill me, while we are en route."

"Afraid of Moy?" Slocum's tongue had grown thick. He had to speak slowly. "Don't take him with you."

"He is my family. All I have left. My honor requires me taking him if he desires to go."

"Insane." Slocum reached for his brandy snifter. He nearly dropped it. The glass felt like a living thing in his hand. "Plain crazy."

"Insane? A sense of family honor? Was not the Confederacy your family, your spiritual family?"

Slocum nodded heavily. There seemed to be logic in what she said. He couldn't think of any arguments. For a second he very seriously, soberly tried to think of an argument. Then his mind flashed with an image

76

of Curly Boyle and his bandy legs loose on a train full of whores, and a wave of laughter shook him.

"How far east did you expect to make it with Curly?"

"Chicago. From there we go north some few hundred miles to a tiny logging community in Wisconsin called Peshtigo. It is a boom town. It is my intention, John Slocum, to sack the town."

With great difficulty, he shook his head, trying to clear it. He couldn't believe he'd heard her right. Wisconsin? Sacking a town? He no longer laughed. His mind swirled. *Sacking?* He tried raising his brandy, but the snifter slithered from his hand. He watched its long fall to the carpet.

"Since you were responsible for Mr. Boyle's death, I now offer you his job. The salary is ten percent of all profits." He looked at her and stared into her eyes. Her eyes were full and wild. "There is a bonus of fifty thousand dollars if you help me kill a man."

Anger boiled deep inside his gut and swelled up through him, burning away the swirling dizziness which had held him. He saw her clearly now. He understood the amber glow that lit her features. It was her dream, her obsession. He slapped her. Not hard—just hard enough to get across his anger. He didn't even stand from the settee, as he struck her. The blow sent her reeling a few steps and brought tears to her eyes. The tears were from shock and astonishment, not pain.

"How dare you strike me!"

"I'm not a pimp, lady. Not a hired killer, not a goddamn butcher. You want to sack a town, find the James boys. Or the Daltons."

Her lips were a mean slash. "No man strikes me." She reached for the bow of her sash.

Slocum leaped and caught her hand as she pulled out the derringer. She tried to scratch him with her free hand. He grabbed both hands and twisted her wrists, prepared to break them like a pair of twigs, until she dropped the gun. It hit the carpet without firing. He pushed her arms behind her back and grasped both of the wrists in his one hand. With his other hand he took hold of her hair, yanking her head back.

"No man strikes you?" he said in a hot whisper. "When was the last time a man did this, bitch?" And he pressed his lips hard against hers.

Her body was tight and ungiving. He released her hair but clamped his fingers onto the nape of her neck. Her struggles became a tremble, whether from fear or passion he neither knew nor cared. He knew he had her now. The sense of his power rushed through him. He forced her close against him and slid a leg between hers, his hard thigh rubbing into her.

She hissed, "My body is scarred."

He took his hand from her neck and reached for her sash. He took hold of the bow, and it was then that the dizziness returned, stronger than before. He felt his strength draining from him. He had the bow in his hand but couldn't pull it. His muscles wouldn't obey his will. He sank and fell; the floor wrapped around him.

Slocum was conscious. Dizzy but conscious. He couldn't move. He could breathe, but his tongue seemed thick and swollen. He couldn't lift an arm, nor a hand, nor even twitch a finger.

Han Su's voice reached him from a far place. "Your cigar. It contained a narcotic. Your muscles are asleep. Your mind and nerves are awake. You can hear. And feel. Feel everything."

Then she was standing above him. She held in her hand the razor with which she had shaved him.

"You struck me, John Slocum. I was wise to take the precaution of drugging you."

She snapped open the razor. The flat of the blade reflected light like a mirror. She bent low and put the tip close to one of his eyes. He could not turn away, ~~~~ ~~~~nk. He saw the finely honed edge of the ~~~~ts bone handle and the thin hand that held

78

it. Above the hand he saw her hard smile. He felt sweat bead his forehead.

Now she straightened up, her feet on either side of his waist. The razor flashed and bounced light as she cut through the sash of her kimono. The silk fell from her with the sound of a slither and she was naked.

"Is this what you hoped to attain by striking me? This scarred body?" She stroked her body as she talked. "I know the scars do not show. To you, this body is lovely. The exotic slant of my features, the mellow hue of my flesh. My breasts, the graceful curve and slope of my hips, the sensuous length of my legs. Men have paid well to have these legs wrapped around them, to have my lips caress them. Is that what you desire? Do you wish to know the mystery and pleasure that lies beneath my mound."

She lay over him. He felt her weight. He felt the cold handle of the razor on his ear, and a cold line of sweat ran from his forehead. She kissed him, pushing her tongue deep in his mouth.

"Perhaps you do not like being kissed against your will, John Slocum. Men have taken me when I have not wanted them. They have paid. All but one has paid dearly."

The razor sliced along his arm and cut through the sleeve of his jacket.

"You struck me. How shall I exact payment from you? Cut out your tongue? Were your tongue not now thick and limp in your throat, I would perhaps sit upon it. It is but one of my scars that that is the only way a man can truly pleasure me."

The razor slashed. Quick cuts sliced away his jacket and shirt. She put a foot on his chest. Her toes flicked away the tatters that covered his torso. Then she went to work on the rest of his clothing. The leather boots took her some time, but when she was through he was naked and the shreds of his clothes lay about him like the skin of a clumsily butchered deer.

She knelt again, straddling his thighs. "Oh, I know

the fear you feel. Your back is frozen with needles of sweat. Your mouth is choked as if full of dust. The worst is not knowing what shall come."

She put the blade against one of her fingers. She cut the finger and drew blood. Holding the cut finger above his chest, she placed the handle of the razor against her dark triangle and slowly bumped her hips. The blade moved like a shimmering, metallic piece of her. She moaned as she bumped and ground her hips. Her writhing hair flailed her shoulders. Her blood dripped, small, hot splashes onto Slocum's chest.

"Imagine yourself a child," she spoke hypnotically, her eyes glazed. "A fourteen-year-old girl. You're on a cot in a tent. The night is hot, but you shiver. You don't know whether you are going to be pawed and raped, or beaten, or preached to. Or perhaps all three. Worst is the waiting. Then the tent flap opens. In your child's vision, the man who lurches through the flap is a giant. He's drunk. But never drunk enough to not hurt you. Maybe tonight you are lucky. Maybe he merely pushes himself into your mouth. This is the quickest way. You know how to make it faster and you don't vomit. He rolls asleep on the cot. You go to a pallet on the ground, afraid of the nightmares that will come if you sleep."

She wrapped her arms around herself. A violent tremor ran through her body. Slocum saw her raise the razor and throw it against a mirror, heard the shatter of glass and the brittle fall of the shards.

"Forget your fears, John Slocum." Her voice was raw and broken. "I will not harm you."

He believed her. He still was unable to move, was still her captive, but in her trembling nudity he saw a wild spirit that had gone too far to go further. She needed rest now. The wildness would return, but now she needed time to herself. The ice that had lined his back began to thaw.

She rubbed a palm in the blood on Slocum's chest. When she spoke, it was more to herself than to him.

80

"My blood is damp and cool. Yet while it courses through me it is hot with hate. My pulse beats with the name of the man who raped me. The man responsible for the death of my family. All except Moy. My blood shall not run cool and sweet through my veins until I have killed the man responsible."

Her eyes were fixed in a rapt stare at her palm, where the blood from her finger had formed a small pool.

"We came as indentured servants to work the construction of the continental railroad. We came shortly before the Civil War. At first, it was not unbearable. Then the war began. A new engineer arrived. He called himself Colonel. He told us the government had placed him in charge of us. What had been twelve-hour shifts became fourteen and soon went to eighteen. Food supplies were cut to less than half. I was to later learn the Colonel was stealing the cut funds for himself. When the workers slowed down from hunger and exhaustion, he brought in supervisors with whips. Those workers who tried to rebel or escape were tortured. Or hanged. And one day the Colonel passed through the cook's tent where I was a cook's assistant. He saw me and ordered me to be in his quarters that night. He read to me from passages of the Gospel and then he raped me."

She paused and knotted her hand that held the small pool of blood into a fist. Blood ran from between her clenched fingers and strained on down her wrist.

"Of my family, only Moy and myself survived. Moy by becoming a supervisor. The most feared of all supervisors. And shortly, it became necessary for him to use opium to forget the things he did for the Colonel. And I, I survived by learning the value of my body. I learned to give what had been taken by force. Every night, in whatever way he wanted me, I was his. Until I at last found my chance and Moy and I escaped. Though I was the younger, it was I who had to control our destinies. I have done well. I have become Madame Lu."

She was silent, staring at the drying blood on her hand and wrist. Slowly, very slowly, she again squeezed her hand into a fist. This time, as her fingers squeezed together, her mouth drew tight as if she were fighting to silence a scream of pain.

"I have lived to kill the Colonel. I traced him to Chicago. Lost him for a while. Recently I learned he is in Peshtigo. John Slocum, you know this man. His name is Marsden."

With the mention of Marsden, Han Su reached out and touched a place on Slocum's neck. She pressed the place and he fell instantly asleep. At least, it was a kind of sleep. He was never to know how much of what happened next was a dream, how much reality. He was adrift in a miasmic flow in which memory and imagination swam together. Hands lifted him and carried him. He found himself in a fresh and green place. Next the black ruins of Marsden's Treachery lay before him. He fought the hands and then was placed on a bed. Or had he fallen there?

Do not try to speak.

The voice rolled over him; it coated him with warm honey and sweet wine. He was in a soft bed in a room with one candle burning. Dark eyes lit with the glow of the forest circled above him. The silver flash of a razor sliced a black curtain.

"Don't speak."

A pair of golden hands caressed his body. He was on a high hill in Tennessee, pillowed in sweet cool grass. Across the night he saw little pockets of flames. A fast-ridden horse bore down on him and a Goliath with a plumed hat leaned down from the saddle. A hollow voice boomed that God causes His wrath to fall upon those who shun Him. The Goliath laughed, and the distant flames flared and swallowed him.

"Let yourself feel pleasure, John Slocum."

82

His flesh was kneaded by golden hands. A firm breast, the size of a pear, filled his mouth. Warm shadows petted him.

"Feel pleasure. Do not speak."

One candle burned. I'm no longer an outlaw, Joe Didion said. I got married. Got a baby, too. Joe chuckled and Curly Boyle, a wounded bird, screeched, "I cain't take it no more!"

"Feel me."

A shadow was moving down his body. Dark hair swished across his belly. He was alive and his cock had grown large and hard and a warm mouth kissed the length of him. His body moved with the shadow, moved in a leisurely rhythm. The shadow shifted, and Han Su, her hips a pale and golden flame, was taking him into her. Their rhythm began again. Unhurried, they moved with the pace set by his waking sensations, every awakening more exquisite. The soft rise and fall of her body quickened him. He stroked the fibrous flesh of her breasts, the heated slope of her hips. He touched the silken place where they were joined, touched the damp, slick hollow. A pleasure he had never known spread through him, a powerful and threatening pleasure, dense and mysterious. He hurried to it, rushed to the pleasure and was taken by it.

A knock at the door brought him awake.

He was alone in bed. Morning sun streamed through the windows. His Colt .44 lay on a bedside table. He took the gun, checked that it was loaded and brought it under the covers before answering the knock.

Two waiters entered. One carried clothing and boots, which he neatly laid out on a chair near the bed. The other wheeled in a breakfast cart. They turned and left without a word.

Slocum felt good with the wide awake freshness of a youth. He also had a youth's hunger. The breakfast cart held juice, coffee, steak, eggs, potatoes and pastry puffs rich with butter. He ate everything.

83

The clothes were identical to those Han Su had slashed off him. He had just finished dressing and was pulling on his boots when, without a knock, she came into the room.

She was wearing the wooden sandals and pale blue cottons commonly worn by women in the Chinese quarter, and she held a pointed straw hat that looked like a basket. The plain clothes boxed her figure.

"I am visiting the ironworks to check upon the progress of my train. Perhaps you would wish to accompany me?"

"What's Marsden doing in Wisconsin?"

"Peshtigo is his town. What he doesn't own, he controls."

"Why didn't you mention Marsden's name instead of drugging me?"

"I am frightened by men I cannot intimidate. The drug put me in control."

"Another scar?"

"Perhaps."

"Don't do it again."

"Do not strike me again." A thin smile of satisfaction played about her lips. "I may assume, then, you are accepting my offer of employment."

"You shouldn't have told me where to find Marsden. I can ride off to Wisconsin and get him without you."

"If you do, I shall have you found. Nor would it be smart business, for you would be losing your share of the profits to be gained on our journey. I will, however, give you the pleasure of the killing. Provided I am there to watch."

"My only job on the trip is protecting you from Moy?"

"Correct. He and I will handle business. He is not to be harmed unless in the defense of me or yourself."

"Sounds easy. Trouble is Moy's a crazy dope addict. And I'm not convinced you're sane."

He went to her. She didn't protest when he took

84

her hat from her hands. As he suspected, her derringer was inside of it.

"Always nice to work for a trusting soul, Han Su."

"You may leave."

"I just might if we don't work out a better deal." He gave her back the hat. He walked away from her and let a few moments pass before saying, "I get a straight fifty percent of all profits. And we will not be *sacking* Peshtigo."

"It is my revenge to destroy everything that is there."

"Your revenge is on Marsden, not a whole goddamn town."

"We will destroy everything that is his."

"Maybe. Logging towns are all backwoods. Usually one road in and out. I want to be damn sure we can get our asses safe out of there. If it looks okay, we'll take the town for what it's worth. Bank, express office, whatever."

"And destroy all that is his?"

Slocum sighed. "Yeah, okay."

"Very well. You shall receive thirty percent."

"Fifty."

"This is my bedroom, John Slocum. I trust you slept with enjoyment. As my protector, you will be with me greatly both night and day. Thirty-five percent."

"I'm surprised Curly Boyle didn't take the job for nothing. Forty percent."

"I would have made different sleeping arrangements for Mr. Boyle. Very well. Forty."

9

The deafening clangor and commotion of the iron-works represented all that Slocum didn't like about cities. It was as crowded as an army camp, but without the military order. Men bumped and shoved one another as they went about their jobs. The air in the yard was thick with dust and grit and foul fumes. Noise assaulted a man's ears: the clang of metal, the crunch of grinding gears, winches screeching like a team of crazed mules. Slocum particularly disliked all the directive signs. "Keep Out." "Danger." "Private." "Authorized Personnel Only." "Keep Right." "No Smoking—Inflammable Area."

"Mr. P.T. Barnum's representative was so impressed by my train, he did not question my price." Han Su had to speak loudly for her voice to carry over the noise of the yard. "He will be meeting us upon our arrival in Chicago."

"Wait a minute," said Slocum. "You're selling your train to Barnum?"

"Once we have arrived in Chicago, the train will serve us no further purpose."

"How about getting to Peshtigo?"

"As you said a short while ago, John Slocum, logging towns are backwoods towns. Marsden is building his own railroad, but the tracks are not yet laid. From Chicago to Peshtigo we shall have to travel either overland by stage or use a water route. I depend on you to choose us the safest means."

Slocum took hold of her arm and stopped her. "I can't protect you if I'm not fully informed."

"But why should my selling my train to Barnum matter to you," smiled Han Su as they began walking again. "After all, the terms of the sale were made previous to our agreement. Therefore, you are not entitled to a share of the profits."

They came to a small, windowless building marked "Authorized Personnel Only." An armed guard stood at the door to enforce the sign. As they entered the building Han Su said, "Once you see my train, you will understand the need for security. Many, such as George M. Pullman or the Union Pacific, would stoop low to learn my designs."

The first thing Slocum saw was a long table covered by a red canvas tarp. The Chinese character that had been on the cards at the Palace, the character meaning hope, was painted in white on the red canvas. There were three men around the table. Two were strangers to Slocum. The third had a familiar round face, gray muttonchops and arthritic hands.

"Howdy, stranger," the third man said with a hearty cheer. "You take my advice 'n ask for the Ruby Twins?"

Slocum nodded. "Morning, Commissioner."

"Heard tell someone fell outta window last night," the Commissioner chuckled. "Damned if I don't sleep through all the good parts."

Han Su said to Slocum, "The Commissioner will be traveling with us, Mr. Green." They had agreed that in the presence of others he would be called Green. There were warrants out for John Slocum in parts of the country they would be crossing. Slocum, when not alone with her, would call her Madame Lu, just like any other employee.

She introduced him to the other men. The first was the architect and designer of her train. Until she had hired him, she said, he had worked as an assistant to the famous George M. Pullman.

"Rescued," the architect said sweetly. "My dear Madame Lu, one was rescued, not hired, from Pullman. That horrendous man's acclaim rests totally upon his abilities to exploit the talents of others. Indeed, the best one may say of him is he possesses an absolute genius for the pecuniary."

"Think I know what you mean," commented Slocum. "Madame Lu's paying you more than Pullman."

The architect didn't hear Slocum's remark. The architect was the type who never heard what wasn't flattering. Slocum promptly forgot his name.

The other man was Mr. Peasly, the engineer, an open and friendly person. He sauntered over to Slocum with an outstretched hand and the gait of a man used to the sway of a rocking train. "Welcome aboard, Mr. Green." His hand was hard with calluses, his grip strong. He wore what looked like a permanent two-day growth of grizzled beard. His nose and cheeks were imbedded with black specks and pitted with tiny pocks, the occupational scars of driving a cinder-spouting engine for a living.

The architect and Mr. Peasly went to the table and very carefully began to roll up the red canvas. As the canvas was rolled back, Slocum saw that the table was a large model. Train tracks ran through rolling green country, past trees, ponds, a water tower, over a river on a bridge and through a tunnel. Slocum had seen similar models, though none quite so elaborate, on construction sites and in the toy departments of big city stores. Then the two men rolled up the remainder of the canvas to reveal the train. He had never, not in the most fanciful flights of his imagination, seen anything like that train.

"Is it not a creation of beauty, Mr. Green?" Han Su said.

"Well." Slocum cleared his throat. "It's bound to be noticed."

"A right circus train, ain't it," chuckled the Commissioner merrily.

The train was a dragon. A garish Chinese dragon. The engine was a dragon's head, with white fangs for a cowcatcher. There was a set of flaring nostrils—Slocum somehow knew they would snort white steam—and pointed nostrils ran back to form the coal car. The sides of the cars were painted to resemble scales. The caboose was a tail—a high, rearing tail—and the whole damn works was splashed with gaudy reds and greens and yellows.

"It pleases me," Han Su said with a mother's pride.

She proceeded to point out the arrangement of the train. Behind the coal and supply cars was the galley. Then came the dining car, followed by the sleeping cars for the girls. Next came the cars where the girls would conduct business. The two gambling cars were separated by a saloon car. Moy's car came next, followed by the caboose.

"My chambers, Mr. Green, shall be the tail."

"The finest element of my design," bragged the architect.

"Notice, Mr. Green," said Han Su, "the manner in which the tail swings up and over the body of the car. It gives me the space of two cars instead of but one."

"My interior staircase," said the architect. "No one has ever used cantilevers as have I."

Slocum said, "You really insist on sleeping there?"

"The observation from the upper level," she said, "will it not be lovely?"

"Probably will," Slocum answered. He pointed to the space behind the coal car. "The view'll look just as good from this spot."

Han Su put a hand to her mouth to cover a polite, ladylike laugh. "Mr. Green, you would have the tail drag the body?"

"Impossible," protested the architect.

"Merely doing what I was hired to do, Madame Lu," said Slocum. "Protecting you."

He glanced at Mr. Peasly. The engineer nodded, his expression showing full agreement with Slocum. The architect, too, knew what Slocum was getting at.

"I assure you," said the architect, "I have taken into consideration all necessary precautions. Notice how the tail tapers outwardly to a bladelike edge. It will glide easily through all oncoming air currents. Notice the open space I have left here between the curving arch of the tail and where it again connects with itself. Crosscurrents shall blow through the opening."

Slocum nodded. "Little top heavy, maybe."

"Without going into details, let us simply say all has been done that may be done. Further, there are times when the esthetics of design must preclude the purely practical."

"That's no doubt news to the Greeks," said Slocum. He reached down and pushed the model train along its tracks. When the train reached the tunnel, Slocum gave the engine an extra little push. At the other end of the tunnel, he caught hold of a car and pushed on toward a rather sharp curve. The dragon's head rounded the curve and continued down the track. The dragon's body had no trouble following its head. The tail fell at the arc of the curve.

"Crash," chuckled the Commissioner.

Slocum said, "It's called whiplash, Madame Lu."

"Mr. Peasly has assured me he can avoid that," she said petulantly.

"Hold on there." Peasly shook his head and scratched his grizzled growth. "Just hold on a sec. What I said was, all things being what they should be, I could avoid it. But if I'm roundin' a bend and get hit by a sudden wind, or if I got to break fast for damn buffalo or somethin' on the track—"

Slocum said, "Only way to make that caboose safe is to cut off the top half of the damn tail. Still wouldn't be doing my job if I let you ride in it. Here's why." He reassembled the train and pushed it up a miniature mountain. He gave the engine a shove when it reached the mountain peak and let gravity carry the train over the crest. Then, just before the tail reached the crest, he flicked the catch that held the caboose to what would be Moy's car. The tail slid partway back down the mountain, toppled over and rolled.

"Crash," said the Commissioner.

Han Su picked up the caboose and looked sadly at it. After a while she said, "What do you suggest, Mr. Green?"

"Give the caboose to Moy. You take his car and move it up here, to behind the galley. That will put the body of the train between you and a possible accident."

"Impossible." The architect stamped his foot. "Each car has been designed as a part of the whole. Shifting a car's position will alter the entire concept."

Slocum looked at the architect. "I'm sure a man of your genius can work it out."

"There simply isn't enough time," the architect protested.

Slocum winked. "Cosmetics."

"Whaaat?"

"A little paint," Slocum said. "Weld a gill here and there. What the hell."

Han Su reluctantly agreed to Slocum's suggestions. The architect protested at length until Han Su quietly mentioned something about salary. Then the man suddenly saw possible ways of making the alterations. Oh, to be sure, he would do them only under protest but—

Han Su wanted interior changes in her new car. Slocum left while she and the architect were discussing them. The Commissioner and Mr. Peasly left with him. The noise of the yard fell on Slocum like a rock slide. He decided to go find a drink and was about to say a friendly good-bye to the two men when the Commissioner produced a flask from his hip pocket.

"What with these knobby hands, stranger, I could use some help twistin' the cap."

Slocum opened the flask and swallowed back a shot. He passed the flask to Mr. Peasly and said, "In a day or so, I'll be wanting a complete tour of the train. I want to know every inch of it before we pull out."

"I'll show you the works, Mr. Green. Not that there's a hell of a lot to see. Despite young Twinkle Toes carryin' on, the real beauty's the engine." He gargled his whiskey like a mouth wash before swallowing it. "Sure glad you got the Madame outta that tail. Goddamn thing's nothin' but a hook waitin' to snag trouble. Weren't fer it, I could get 'nother five, maybe ten miles an hour speed from my engine."

The Commissioner took a swig from the flask. "Mr. Peasly's so all fired proud over his engine he's goin' along with it to Barnum."

"Wouldn't feel right turnin' it over to someone else," said Peasly. "Course I'd rather be carryin' passengers an' mail 'stead of a bunch of damn elephants and jugglers. Then again, I never figured I'd one day be carryin' a trainload o' Hooker's girls."

"Old Joe Hooker. Let's drink to him." The Commissioner chuckled. He swallowed another shot and passed the flask to Slocum. "Hooker weren't much of a general to President Lincoln, but he sure did add to the language."

"How's that?" asked Peasly.

"Hell, Mr. Peasly, I thought ev'ryone knew. Old Joe figured a fightin' man was a fuckin' man, wanted his boys to get laid the night 'fore a battle. While's other officers, North an' South, tried gettin' rid of the camp followers, Hooker welcomed them, so nat'rally the girls took to followin' his troops. They got to be known as Hooker's girls. Now days some folks just call 'em hookers." The flask had come around to the Commissioner again. He drank and passed it on. "Yessir, changin' the language ain't a bad legacy. You agree, stranger?"

"Commissioner," said Slocum. "Just what the hell are you commissioner of?"

"Oh, I'm an ex," the man chuckled. Since taking his last shot, his veined nose had reddened. "Ex-Commissioner of Sanitation. Me 'n the city council, we had a disagreement over some missing funds."

"Way I heard it, them funds weren't never missing," said Mr. Peasly. He gargled down a shot. "Way I heard it, you knew where they was all the while."

"Rumors, Mr. Peasly. Politics, stranger. A mendacious marriage." He laughed. "The hell of it is, now nobody's collectin' the garbage."

The engineer said he had work to do and left them. The Commissioner put the flask near his ear and shook it. "Not much left. Might as well finish it." He had a shot and passed the flask. "You're likely wonderin' what I'm doin' on this little jaunt?"

"Baby-sitting the Ruby twins?" asked Slocum.

The Commissioner doubled over laughing. A hearty

paroxysm of laughter shook him until he was out of breath and coughing. He wiped the corners of his eyes with the enlarged knuckles of a hand. His bulb of a nose was bright as a cherry. "Stranger, you make me feel like I was sixty again."

"Why *are* you making this trip?"

"Madame Lu wants me along. Thinks my political expertise can be of help in some o' the places we'll be stoppin'. Me bein' a man, she figures I'll be able to bribe the local law quicker 'n cheaper than she çan. Least it's what she claims. Might be she's repayin' me what she thinks she owes. I jumped at the chance. Figure my heart's due to blow up soon, or my kidneys spring a leak. I want a last fling. Here! Last swallow's yours."

Slocum finished the whiskey. "What would she be repaying you for?"

"When I ran the sanitation department I gave a lot o' her people jobs. I could've stole ten times what they say I stole an' it wouldn't have hurt me much as hirin' them Chinese. They're a shit-upon group. Since gettin' the railroad built, most people, the good people, want to get rid o' the Chinese. They've managed to write legislation so's a Chinaman can't stake a claim, can't buy or own much more than his socks. Can't even pick up the garbage no more. Hate to think what'll happen to them. Up to now, ev'ry Monday Madame Lu sent a wagon of food, clothes and money to the Chinese quarter. Guess the poor bastards'll just starve."

"If she's so damned concerned about her people," said Slocum, "why doesn't she employ them?"

"They won't work anywhere near Moy. Chinese are proud. Strong sense of honor. They'd rather starve than come near him. Guess you realize, stranger, you're goin' to have to face down Moy."

"Maybe not."

The Commissioner cocked his head and scratched his muttonchops. "It's why you were hired. Madame Lu's bankin' you'll have to kill him to keep him from killing you. That way, it won't be murder, and her sense of honor will be secure."

A few times Slocum wondered just what the hell he was getting himself into—Moy, Han Su, a trainload of whores, half the country to cross—and he considered chucking the whole deal and riding off to Wisconsin alone. Then he would think about the money to be made on the trip, which would be sizable, according to Slocum's thinking. And, he would think about Han Su's golden body.

That night he and Han Su had dinner together in her chambers. After eating, they spread out the maps and looked them over. Han Su had a number of places where she planned to stop, though they would also be pulling over at any little siding that looked ripe for some action. Their layovers would last from a night to a week, depending on the business and the local law. They would reach Peshtigo by October, giving them sufficient time to do their job and clear out before a storm could snowbound them for the winter.

Peshtigo was Slocum's main concern. It was a new town and the maps didn't give much information. The place was surrounded by forest, and Slocum saw only two ways in and out. The getting in was no problem. They could go overland by wagon, or they could sail up Lake Michigan, through Green Bay and on up the Peshtigo River. But the overland routes merged into a single road for the last forty miles. Too many miles for an escape route. And he certainly didn't like the idea of trying to escape by boat.

"Do you have contacts in Chicago?" he asked.

"All over the country I have contacts."

"I want an Indian. One from the Peshtigo area. One who hates Marsden for cutting down the forests."

"I do not understand."

"Just find me an Indian."

10

A goldfish pool was in the foyer of the first floor of the Palace of Pleasure. The pool was a long and shallow rectangle, and its surface, due to the flickering reflections of the gas lamp, resembled a rippled mirror. Slocum avoided walking here—he didn't like the hollow echo the stone floor of the foyer gave to his boot heels, nor did he care for the wavy, eerie reflections cast from the surface of the pool—but it was here, a few nights before the train left San Francisco, that Slocum had an encounter with Moy.

Slocum approached Moy from the opposite side of the pool, but both Moy and his sidekick Hip Sing were so engrossed in what they were doing that they didn't hear Slocum's approach. They were feeding the goldfish; Moy watched while Hip Sing threw handfuls of silver minnows into the pool. Moy was nodding, as if half asleep. His hands were folded into his sleeves and his jeweled pigtail snaked down over his crossed arms.

"Evening," Slocum called from across the pool, his voice echoing dully.

"Ah, Mr. Green." Moy bowed. "Do you also find fish a relaxing sight?"

"Only in a frying pan."

"Watch with us, please," Moy said.

Moy's rouged lips stretched with a tight grin as Hip Sing threw out another handful of minnows. Hip Sing's mouth was partially open. There was a sheen of sweat on his forehead and his hips rocked slightly.

The goldfish schooled and swirled the water and greedily fed on the tiny minnows. One fish, nearly the size of a trout, took a half-dozen minnows in a single mouthful. A minnow became trapped between the orange jaws of the large fish. The minnow bucked and twisted. The fish opened its mouth to take in the minnow, but the minnow swam free. The freed minnow then desperately attempted to swim to safety. It went to the bottom of the pool and sought shelter under the cover of a flat, decorative stone. The large goldfish lazily followed the minnow, nudged aside the stone and swallowed its trapped prey.

"Aighhh!" Hip Sing cried with excitement. His shrill cry echoed like a shiver.

"Is this not interesting, Mr. Green?" Moy asked.

Slocum pointed to the center of the pool. "What's wrong with that black one?"

"Old," said Moy with a shrug. His motion created a slither that ran the length of his pigtail. "About to die. Too weak to feed itself. Watch."

Hip Sing threw some minnows over the sick fish. It's black body was already swollen with approaching death and the other goldfish pushed it out of the way and took the minnows. The sick fish bobbed to the surface and floated with a weakly flipping tail.

"I should put it out of misery," said Moy. "Unfortunately, it swims beyond my reach."

"Want me to shoot it?"

"You Westerners place such importance upon your noisy bullets, as if death must come with the sound of thunder. Yet the fine silk mesh of a butterfly net is able to capture and silence a bullet."

"Once at a circus," said Slocum, "I saw a fellow catch a bullet in a net. Figured it was a trick."

"No stunt, I assure you." Moy shook his head, and his pigtail slithered. His reflection rippled over the surface of the water. "You notice the smooth flat stones decorating the bottom of the pool? A bullet would bounce off them, yet Hip Sing is capable of breaking them with the blade of his hand."

"The same fellow in the same circus did that trick, too. Standing next to him was a better act. Trained fleas."

Hip Sing piped shrilly, "You insult us."

"Mr. Green meant no insult," said Moy. "Mr. Green is now a member of our family. He would not bring disharmony among us by making an insult." Moy removed his hands from his sleeves. His fingers were long and smooth, the nails filed to points and glistening with clear lacquer. He opened his arms and bowed low. The reflections of his hands floated over the water like pale gulls about to swoop. "I welcome you to our family."

"I'm just a hired man," said Slocum. He attempted to look up the sleeves of Moy's open arms, hoping to see if there actually were cleavers hidden, but the folds of the man's smock concealed his arms.

"You have aligned yourself with my cousin, Madame Lu. Thus you have aligned yourself with me." Moy brought a hand to his chest. "My heart was heavy with sadness until I learned of this alignment. I was sad because only recently I lost a devoted member of my family. He, like Humpty Dumpty, had a great fall. All the king's men could do nothing. My grievous heart wept at the loss of his loyalty and devotion. But now, now I am again happy, for you have come to take his place."

"Sounds like you and this Humpty Dumpty were real close."

"Like brothers, Mr. Green." Moy put his hands back inside his sleeves. "But we go on. You have taken his place in our family and we go on. Soon we begin an immense journey. Long and arduous. Many unforeseen events may befall us—hardships, misfortune, perhaps death. Should such a tragedy befall us, we who survive will go on. It is the nature of tragedy to strengthen and unite those who share grief. Is that not curious?"

"Yep," said Slocum. His own reflection was a long, wavering shadow on which the sick fish limply swam. "Curious as money in the pocket of an honest man. Which reminds me, I'll be keeping a close eye on the gambling cars."

"That is for us to do," piped Hip Sing.

"But of course I welcome your eyes," said Moy. "But to what purpose?"

97

"I don't want some mule skinner getting the mistaken idea he's being dealt a crooked hand. Mule skinners lose face easily. They form lynch mobs."

"You are of my family, thus your wishes must be met. However, I feel I must warn you of one who is not of us. The notorious outlaw, John Slocum. One of our employees told me she encountered him on a recent night. I convinced her of the wisdom of not repeating her tale, Mr. Green. In truth, I believe she was under an illusion. I sincerely hope she was, as I would never wish to meet John Slocum."

"That's very wise, Moy. From what I've heard, this Slocum is one mean sonofabitch." Slocum turned and started away. He had taken only a few steps when he heard a faint, quick whir and the splash of water. He spun around.

The sick goldfish was no longer suffering. It lay at the bottom of the pool, anchored by the weight of the cleaver that had killed it.

11

All of San Francisco turned out to see Madame Lu and her train depart. People from the rest of California turned out also. Plus: foreign seamen ashore from ships anchored in the harbor, a few foreign dignitaries, some Indians who had trekked into town for the occasion, snake oil drummers, tin pot salesmen, gimcrack vendors, farmers, politicians, clergymen, cowboys, clerical workers, barbers, whores, ironworkers, housewives—the elegant and the impoverished, the sleazy and the pristine. Some came to praise the departing madame, some to bury the fleeing vixen, but most were there for the biggest party since statehood.

Helium-filled balloons floated in the air. Eight bands of musicians played for the crowd. Dogs barked. Firecrackers exploded.

Barrels of drink were quaffed: beer, imported wine,

island rums, fruit punches, bonded whiskeys and whiskeys bottled yesterday. The food was everything from roast prairie hen to broiled whale steak, caviar served from swan-shaped blocks of ice to Texas barbecue plus sour pickles, baked hams, kumquats in honey, baked beans, smoked fish, codfish cakes, melons, charred chunks of buffalo, ice cream and sweet pastries.

Four barbershop quartets sang. The mayor of Frisco presented Madame Lu with a bouquet. A diva from the opera house sang.

The crowd cheered as someone rode through on a camel. A race between the camel and a quarter horse was quickly organized. The camel won.

A monk from the Chinese quarter sprinkled the dragon's head with water and blessed the train.

The British consul gave Madame Lu a silver tea service. The French consul gave her a set of dueling pistols.

A twelve-boy choir sang. The Ruby twins sang.

A magician went about changing apples into oranges, pulling endless lengths of silk from his sleeves, and finding birds and coins in little boys' ears.

Madame Lu's girls threw small presents to the little girls. Party favors, lipsticks, tins of rouge, garters.

A Polynesian man in a grass skirt danced with knives. A mountain man danced with a bear.

The Commissioner complained about his gout and kissed all the ladies.

A Russian admiral gave Madame Lu a baby seal. A German captain presented her with a German shepherd puppy. Madame Lu passed the animals to her girls and told them to make suitable accommodations. The girl who had been with Curly in the playroom suite took the seal. She wrapped her arms around the sleek, black body. The seal barked and lathered her cheeks with a pink tongue. She gave up the seal for ten minutes, the time it took for her to do a baton twirling act. She maneuvered two silver batons at once as silver cords spun from the points of her sequined bra.

The state militia drill team marched. Bagpipes from the police department Emerald Society performed.

A Catholic priest sprinkled the dragon's head with water and blessed the train.

Slocum got into the spirit of things. While the Commissioner threw cinders into the air, Slocum drew his gun and blasted them to dust.

And during the whole time of the party, seldom did a full minute pass without the whistle of the dragon being heard—a high, siren whistle, frivolous and mad, with the strength of a thousand bugles. The dragon's nostrils bellowed and steam mushroomed above the train, drifting and settling upon the cars. Wet sheen glistened the dragon's scales. The lurid colors pulsed. The dragon breathed.

They had been scheduled to leave at noon. Four hours later Slocum took Han Su aside and told her it was time to move out. Her dark eyes were ablaze with pride. Slocum doubted she had noticed the passage of time. He was surprised when she didn't protest their leaving.

She merely said, "This is but the beginning, John Slocum."

The Commissioner refused to get aboard. He insisted on tagging along beside Slocum and helping get everyone on the train. But he wasn't the greatest of help because he stopped at every other car to have a *bon voyage* drink with old friends.

They finally made it to the dragon's tail. Most of the day's action had centered around the head, but there was a sizable crowd here. Neither Moy nor Hip Sing were among the crowd. But the side door of the caboose was open and the scent of opium wafted from it.

"In the caboose," shouted Slocum. "Ready to move?"

Moy appeared at the door. His hands were hidden in his sleeves, his eyes popped in a glassy stupor. His stance was crooked, almost drunken. The contrast between the bright sunlight and the dim interior of the caboose appeared to have affected his vision. He scowled and squinted.

"Ah, Mr. Green." Moy bowed. His thin body teetered half out the door and he looked like he might fall. A black-gloved hand reached from the dark interior of the caboose and pulled him up. Then the hand disappeared; Slocum hadn't seen who Moy's rescuer had been. "Hip Sing, I fear, has one piece of luggage yet to arrive with," Moy said.

"He's got ten minutes," said Slocum.

"His delay, I am sure, is due only to the immensity of the crowd." Moy weaved back and forth. His rouged lips spread like a streak of oil. "It has been a day of great merriment, a portent of the joy and prosperity that await our dragon. This small delay of Hip Sing gives me opportunity to present my new good friends."

Two men joined Moy at the open door, one on each side of him. Their presence widened the spread of his oily smile.

"What the fuck," muttered the Commissioner. "Moy recruitin' freaks for Barnum?"

"This is my good friend, Marquez," said Moy with a nod toward the man with the reputation.

Marquez had the hooked nose of a bird of prey and his hair hung in thin, greasy braids. His reputation was known to Slocum. He wore a gun, but the reputation wasn't based on his ability to shoot. Throughout the Southwest, Marquez was known as the Knife. There was a skinning knife sheathed to each of his boots. Two bowies were strapped to his waist. A bandoleer crossed his chest, but instead of bullets, the bandoleer held a dozen slim daggers. The hilt of another knife was visible behind his neck.

"And this is Mr. Cranshaw," said Moy.

The stocky Cranshaw was the black-gloved man. He wore a brace of guns Texas-style. A beard the color of

101

gray mud didn't quite hide the part of his jaw that had been shot away.

"My friends are your friends, Mr. Green," said Moy. "We are all good friends."

Slocum heard the piping voice of Hip Sing behind him. "Much hurry! Quickly! This way! This way!"

He turned to see Hip Sing pushing through the crowd. The Chinaman was followed by someone who looked more like a fleshy rock than a man. The follower carried a steamer trunk.

"Ahhh," said Moy. "Here we have another new friend. He who carried the heavy burden of my luggage is named Lumbar."

Hip Sing scurried to the open caboose and slapped the floor. "Here! Put trunk here."

Lumbar sluggishly approached the caboose. He moved as if each step required an effort of thought. He flung the trunk like a sack of leaves and it slammed down heavily against the floor of the caboose.

Moy said, "You must meet Mr. Green, Lumbar."

A moment passed while Lumbar appeared not to have heard Moy, and Moy repeated his statement. Moy was about to repeat himself yet a third time when Lumbar took a step forward and attempted to look inside the caboose.

"No there!" Hip Sing put a hand on Lumbar and guided him around and pointed to Slocum. "There he!"

Lumbar had the blank smile of an overfed baby. He was short, no more than five foot five, but he was almost as wide. His arms were shaped like clubs and damn near hung to his knees. His head seemed twisted into his shoulders like a cap screwed on a canteen. His eyes were pink buttons set deep in his forehead. He had bare feet, probably because he couldn't find boots large enough. He wore no gun.

Slocum turned to the Commissioner. "What do you think?"

"Looks like Moy's armed hisself with a gun, a knife an' a muscle."

102

"Not much point in waiting," said Slocum.

"You ain't thinkin' of takin' on all three?" asked the Commissioner.

Slocum removed his gun belt and handed it to the Commissioner. "I'd appreciate you shooting anybody who might interfere."

The Commissioner clumsily pulled the Colt from its holster. "Damn knobby fingers ain't much good at pullin' triggers."

"Maybe they don't know that."

The bystanders sensed a fight. They grew quiet, pulled back and opened up some room. The cleared space was approximately fifteen square feet of cinder-covered ground, and Slocum stepped into the center of it.

"Hip Sing," said Slocum, "get on the train."

"Quickly, Hip Sing," said Moy. His voice was beginning to crack with a giggle. "Mr. Green is most anxious to get started."

Lumbar watched Hip Sing climb into the caboose. He looked dumbly from Moy to Slocum, waiting for someone to tell him what to do.

Slocum hunkered down, scooped up cinders and rubbed them between his palms. He motioned for Lumbar to join him.

Cinders crunched beneath Lumbar's feet as he made his way to Slocum. When he squatted near Slocum, the backs of his hands were against the ground. His bent knees were the size of spades, and his scrunched-in head was almost lost between the thick blocks of his shoulders.

"Lumbar," said Slocum. "You don't want to go on any train trip.

Lumbar's pink eyes blinked. He grunted.

"Just say good-bye, Lumbar."

Lumbar grunted.

"You do know how to say good-bye?" Slocum was counting on Lumbar being slow. He knew he didn't stand much of a chance if Lumbar caught him in those

103

arms. "Or do you just grunt, Lumbar? Like a fucking dummy?"

A dim light went on in Lumbar's pink eyes. He reached for Slocum, and at that instant Slocum sprang to his feet. At the same time, he threw a handful of cinder grit into Lumbar's eyes. Lumbar's hands clapped together on empty air. His massive weight carried him forward and he nearly toppled. Slocum kept Lumbar from toppling by kicking him solidly in the jaw.

The kick lifted Lumbar. He staggered backward, arms flailing as he attempted to stop his backward thrust.

Slocum knotted his hands into a double-fist and charged before Lumbar could recover. He smashed Lumbar's windpipe. Lumbar gagged, and as he struggled for air, Slocum shot fast punches into his belly. The belly blows had no effect, and Slocum continued them a moment too long. Lumbar managed to hook a hand under Slocum's left arm, lift him off his feet and toss him to the ground.

Slocum rolled well out of Lumbar's reach. Half the wind had been knocked out of him. Gasping for breath, he got to his feet and waited for Lumbar to make the next move.

Lumbar was holding his injured throat, coughing and spitting up blood; his eyes had darkened into round red spots. Then he began to circle Slocum, his arms swinging from their sockets like hanging hams. He wasn't wild. He was slow and awkward, but not wild. Slowly, he tightened the circle. Once he faked a rush, but Slocum didn't go for it.

"Crush 'im, Lumbar," someone called from the caboose.

Slocum didn't look to see whether it was Cranshaw or Marquez who had called. He kept his attention on Lumbar, who faked another rush. Then Lumbar dug his bare toes into the cinders, bracing himself, and that clued Slocum to the real move. He held steady as Lumbar charged. A hair before Lumbar reached him,

puppy; it was finally decided Burger had the right sound—Germanic without being too Teutonic. The seal ended up with the handle Trixie's Gleason—Trixie being the name of the girl from the playroom suite. Slocum never did learn where the hell Gleason came from. Following the naming, the Commissioner, armed with a Bible, his most officious tone and a Ruby twin at either elbow, swore in the animals as official mascots of the train.

Madame Lu, dressed in her finest silks, was seated in a special chair near the bar. She was radiant with pleasure. Slocum had never seen her so damn relaxed, so open. Gone was all but a trace of her usual regal composure. Even in the bed they shared, no matter the abandon with which she gave her body, there was always a certain holding back. Not from him, but from herself. Tonight, though, she was free and personable. She laughed with the girls as if she were one of them, kissing each of them affectionately on the cheek.

She almost wept when presented with a patchwork quilt the girls had made themselves. Almost, but not quite. Her voice cracked when she made a thank-you speech. She spoke with confusion and uncustomary haste; but at the last moment, before a tear could fall, she blinked and recovered. A few minutes later she, Slocum and the Commissioner went forward to the dining car.

Their supper was a chilled poached fish embedded in an orange aspic, which trembled with the rhythm of the train. Ice rattled in a bucket containing a bottle of white wine. Small waves of wine splashed inside their glasses. Silver rattled. Salt and pepper mills shook. And just outside the window the wooded California landscape passed silently and smoothly.

Han Su lifted her wine glass in toast. "To Wisconsin."

"Eastward, ho!" added the Commissioner. His round features were ruddy with high cheer, but a weary slump of his shoulders showed that the day's merriment had begun to take its toll.

Slocum didn't care much for the meal. Neither did the Commissioner, judging by the expression on his face. He kept adding salt, and his twisted hands had trouble holding the shaker. With every lurch of the train, salt sprinkled his vest like falling dandruff. Eventually he gave up and settled back with the wine, which he complained was too cold and hurt his teeth. Han Su had withdrawn since the girls' presentation of the quilt. She sat stiffly, as if she were alone, eating with small deliberate bites.

Slocum asked, "How many on this train know Wisconsin is our final destination?"

"Only but the three of us and Moy," answered Han Su. "The others all believe Chicago."

"A few more parties like today and news of us will get to Wisconsin," said Slocum.

"But the train stops in Chicago, Mr. Green."

"You were posing for photographers today, Madame Lu. Supposing a tintype reached Wisconsin?"

Han Su slowly chewed a bite of jellied fish. "I have changed much in the years since I was last seen by our quarry."

Slocum glanced at the Commissioner. He wasn't sure how much the man knew about Wisconsin. "What about Moy?"

"Moy has a superstitious fear of the magic box," said Han Su. "He would not allow his photograph to be taken."

The Commissioner chuckled, a strangled tone in his voice. "Only thing ever changes 'bout Moy is his pigtail. Keeps addin' jewels."

"And you, Mr. Green?" said Han Su. "Were you not also seen by our quarry?"

"Only in the dark." Slocum drained his glass and leaned back in his chair. "Maybe Moy should cut his hair."

Han Su turned a cool glance to Slocum. "I will not allow it."

"If Moy can be recog—"

108

"Never!" Han Su raised her voice. Her expression looked as though it had been carved from ice. "Do you understand me, Mr. Green?"

"Be like cuttin' his balls, stranger," the Commissioner said. "A Chinaman's braid is a prideful thing."

Slocum smiled. "Staying alive is mighty prideful to me."

Han Su, with a slow and calculated gesture, laid her utensils down on the table. She pursed her lips, and her voice became hard and brittle as she said, "Mr. Green, do you deliberately seek to insult my family? I understand you beat unmercifully a companion of Moy's."

"It was him or me," responded Slocum.

"Did you not provoke the fight?"

"Moy hired on three men. Their purpose was to get me. Now he's only got two. Plus Hip Sing."

"No need to worry on Hip Sing." The Commissioner wiped his forehead with a napkin. "Hip Sing's a mere popinjay. Chirps to Moy's command. Fills his pipe an' keeps his fires."

Han Su interrupted. "You do not know for certain why those men were hired."

"True," said Slocum. "They may have been hired to get you."

"You need not be facetious," she snapped.

"When I came in," continued Slocum, "we had a ground rule. I wasn't to touch cousin Moy unless he came at you or me. I haven't."

"I do not question the integrity of your word, Mr. Green." She turned from him before adding, "Merely your method."

"My method, *madame,* is to force Moy's hand."

"Want Moy to show his hand?" The Commissioner threw down his napkin with a gruff laugh. "Step on Hip Sing's toes. Moy'll be the one to shout."

"Enough!" Han Su silenced the Commissioner with a clap of her hands. "I do not wish to pursue this line of discussion."

The Commissioner bristled. He glowered across the table, his features red and dripping sweat. Han Su glared at him until he settled back in his chair, a sullen expression covering his face.

Then she smiled. It wasn't a pleasant smile. She primly and politely said, "More fish, gentlemen?"

Slocum stood up from his chair. He said to the Commissioner, "Stay with the madame until I get back."

Slocum went through the train until he reached Han Su's private car. In the corridor, he carefully placed his ear against the door and listened. Nothing. He unlocked the door and eased it open, reaching out to catch the small feather drifting down from the top of the door, where he had placed it earlier. Any professional entering the car would have noticed the feather; it was a common enough method of spotting an intrusion. A professional would have caught the feather and replaced it, but while doing all that he would have been too busy to notice the soft crunch of the fragments of eggshells Slocum had put beneath the rug.

Slocum lifted the rug. The shells weren't broken. Still, he started through the car checking to see that nothing was disturbed or missing.

He had taken only a few steps when an eerie feeling slid through him. Someone had been here. Everything appeared to be where it was supposed to be, nothing was missing, but someone had entered and left. He knew it. He stood a moment, his long legs moving with the rocking motion of the train, wondering whether his imagination was playing tricks on him. The windows were all locked. The eggshells were unbroken. But he knew it wasn't his imagination. An intruder had gone through this car.

He began looking for evidence of the intrusion. He opened all the closets, the cabinets, the chests. He lifted cushions and looked behind drapes. Nothing—except that the packing behind a mirror appeared to have been disturbed: a bit of cotton-fleece packing was

110

caught between the thin backpiece and the framework. But it wasn't conclusive; he hadn't checked the back of the mirror earlier and the fleece might have always been exposed. Or the movers could have exposed it. Anyway, what would someone be searching for there?

He braced his arms against a window frame and looked out at the fleeting black forms of the night. It would help, he thought ruefully, if he knew what it was the intruder had been seeking. He happened to be glancing down when he found his evidence—a scratch in the highly polished lacquer at the base of the window and small flecks of wax near the window bolt.

Proof of the intrusion raised more questions. Why? What had the intruder wanted? And perhaps more important: had he found it? Outside, the black shadows of the passing trees offered no answer. He would have to look elsewhere. He scooped up the eggshells and the feather and left the car.

He went to the open walkway behind the car. The noise of the engine reached him like a grinding, distant echo, and he was very aware of the smell of soot and oil. He tossed the eggshells to the wind. They were no longer needed. Then he looked down and saw the silver blur of the nearest wheels and the black rush of the roadbed. Only a few, but treacherous inches separated Han Su's car from the one adjoining. Safety straps connecting the cars snapped and rattled at the bolts. The separate ends of each car's curved walkway lunged and shifted, back and forth, like toothless gears attempting to mesh.

Slocum stepped across to the other car. He took hold of a narrow, steel ladder that was at the side of the car and climbed it.

The wind hit him in the back as he climbed on top of the train. The noise of the engine was all but swallowed by the wind in his ears. It was a warm, damp wind—the kind that blows before a rainstorm. There was no moon, no stars visible in the vast dark sky above. Lamps burned from many of the windows, their pale light spilling down to the rushing ground. Sparks from the engine flew about him like fireflies, though even this tiny bit of light was denied him as the sparks sizzled and extinguished against the dew-slick surface of the roof. Dim and distant at the rear of the train were the lamps of the dragon's rising tail.

He moved in a low crouch, his feet wide apart to keep balance with the swaying of the train. He walked with a slow, rolling gait that was almost a crawl. The hardest part was leaping over the black space between cars, that moment of suspension when the roar of the wind seemed to subside and he heard instead the more subtle thunder-roll of the wheels.

After a half-dozen leaps he began to move more quickly. Soon he had gone far enough so that the engine sparks could no longer reach him. The caboose, the rising tail, was nearer.

He reached the saloon car. The girls were still partying. Their windows were open and their laughter trailed into the night. He was almost across the saloon car when the train suddenly slowed, and he was thrown off balance. He fell. His knees cracked against the roof. Unable to grasp onto the dew-wet surface, he threw himself flat and hugged the roof to keep from rolling off.

The train had slowed for a curve. A hairpin curve. For an instant the dragon's head was directly opposite him. It cut a fierce outline against the sky. Mr. Peasly stood at his controls. His features burned with flames reflected from his engine. He reached up and pulled a cord. White steam gushed from the dragon's nostrils. A shrill whistle entered the night.

Slocum pressed down hard as the saloon car rounded the curve. He watched the caboose turn the curve. The tail tilted but the angle wasn't dangerous. The caboose was in no danger of leaving the track, but Slocum felt he was seeing the form of an unreal beast. The whistle was still in his ears when a streak of lightning cracked. The tail glistened. A shimmer of green and yellow lit the tail. Then it began to rain.

Slocum moved on. The train was again at high speed. The rain had started to seep through his clothes. He paused before leaping across to the caboose.

Light streamed from all the windows. None were open. The wide arch of the tail rose above the rear half of the car. Moy and his men could be in the arch. They could be in the lower level or spread throughout the whole damned thing. He had to get over to the caboose without alarming them.

The rain fell harder. Another streak of lightning lit the slick roof of the caboose. In the brief moment of the flash, Slocum saw how he could cross to the opposite roof.

From its arch, the tail dipped back to the roof with a narrowing line, then curved up again. The tip of the tail was no thicker than a gun barrel. It bounced up and down like a spring and looked about as sturdy as a young girl's wrist.

He wasn't about to turn back, not after coming this far. He jumped and caught hold of the tip, praying it was stronger than it looked.

It was. It took the force of his leap, and he dropped lightly to the roof.

He paused for an instant, listening for some sound from the caboose below. Wind and rain were all he heard. And the roll of wheels, the low constant rolling.

He inched his way along the roof until he reached the first window of the arch. The darkness of the night aided him now. As he edged up to look through the window, he knew anyone inside the lit interior would have difficulty seeing him. But no one was inside the arch. And he cursed his luck, because if they weren't in the arch they had to be below, and there was only one way to look in the lower windows.

He pulled his gun and shoved it between his belt and belly. It was damned uncomfortable, but he didn't want

113

to risk its sliding from his holster while he was hanging over the side of the caboose.

Slocum was soaked to the skin now. The wind was cold; an extra icy chill went through him as he lay flat and began to lower himself. The little raised surfaces of the dragon's scales offered him handholds. The holds were sharp-edged and wet, and by the time he had lowered himself far enough to see through a window, his legs were only precariously hooked to the roof.

They were all there in a little cluster. It was like an ornate sitting room inside; the decor Han Su had chosen for herself had never been altered to match another's personality. The two cowboys, Marquez and Cranshaw, looked absurdly out of place amid all the frills. Marquez was brooding over a chess board, his greasy braids bobbing in and out, moving chess pieces with an imaginary opponent. Cranshaw stood in the center of the car. He was drinking from a bottle and lurching drunkenly with the sway of the train. Hip Sing squatted near a thronelike chair.

Moy lazed in the chair, his sandaled feet resting on the steamer trunk Lumbar had loaded. Beside his feet were a globeless burning lamp, a wooden-handled needle, and a small pot containing some sort of gray substance. Moy's eyes were closed. In one hand he held a long thin-stemmed pipe. His other hand was stroking Hip Sing's hair.

Rain lashed Slocum's face and streaked the window through which he peered. His gun bit into his belly. He heard the wheels rushing along beneath him and he tightened his hands on his hold.

Inside the car, Cranshaw waved the bottle and said something that brought a smile to Marquez's lips. Moy opened his eyes. He stared with contempt at Cranshaw and moved his hand in a slow caress along Hip Sing's cheek. Hip Sing curled in with the touch, as Moy sucked on his pipe. Then Moy frowned, examined the bowl and spoke to Hip Sing.

Hip Sing immediately picked up the needle on the

114

steamer trunk and placed it in the flame of the lamp. Keeping the wooden handle between the palms of his hands, he rapidly spun the needle until half its length glowed with red heat. Then, still spinning the needle between his palms, he dipped its tip into the gray substance in the small pot. Within seconds a ball had formed on the needle tip. He lifted the needle into the flame and spun it until the ball became pink and looked about to melt; then, deftly, he dropped it into Moy's pipe.

Moy puffed. He made a wave of his hand that brought a pleased expression to Hip Sing's face.

Cranshaw threw back his head with a drunken laugh and raised the bottle to his lips. He nearly toppled backward as he drank and emptied the bottle. He shook the empty bottle, then lurched out of Slocum's sight.

As Slocum stretched to keep Cranshaw in view, one of his hands slipped from its hold. He struggled to regain the hold. His hand slid along the slippery surface. His fingers couldn't get a grip on anything. Lightning flashed. He saw the hard speeding ground as his arm flailed into space. His legs began to slide from the roof. The weight of his dangling arm was pulling him over the edge. Rain filled his eyes and blurred his vision. His dangling arm reached for something, anything; his other hand fought to keep its hold. He continued to slide. A leg plunged off the edge, taking half his body with it. His dangling hand scraped over the jutting frame of the window. He jammed his palm against a corner of the frame and felt a sudden piercing sensation. His palm was pierced. He ignored the pain and stiffened his arm, stopping his slide. He kicked back with his leg. His boot caught a toehold on the shallow eave of the roof.

The side door, only a yard from where he struggled to keep from falling, slid open and an empty bottle went sailing into the night.

Slocum pressed down hard on his palm; the window frame bit deeper into it. His other hand still held its original hold, but his fingers were stiff with tension. He could hear the movement of the men inside the caboose.

"You'll never hit it, amigo," Marquez said. "Too far away by now."

Cranshaw muttered, "The fuck I can't."

Then suddenly Cranshaw was leaning out the door, a gun in his hand. His back was to Slocum as he fired two shots in the direction the bottle had sailed. Slocum held himself rigidly, afraid to move, afraid the slightest sound he made would cause Cranshaw to spot him.

"Bottle all gone!" shouted Hip Sing. "Close door quickly!"

"Fuck you," Cranshaw grumbled. He fired another two rounds. "I like the air."

"Opium fumes get escaping!" cried Hip Sing. "No good lose fumes."

Blood from the palm Slocum had pressed against the window frame began to leak a rain-tinted streak down the window. The fingers of his other hand were numb. Then the train hit a bump and he almost lost his precious toehold on the roof. As he thrust to save his toehold, his numb fingers began to slip.

"Close door now!" shouted Hip Sing while leaping to his feet and running from Slocum's line of vision.

Cranshaw growled, "You slant-eyed fairy." A moment later Hip Sing went through the air and landed back where he had started from. Cranshaw came back into Slocum's view and went for the fallen Chinaman.

"Sit down, Mr. Cranshaw," Moy ordered coolly. Cranshaw muttered something inaudible as he went to a seat, and Hip Sing put his head against Moy's legs and cried noisily.

Slocum was slipping. He had to chance that Hip Sing's crying would keep them from hearing him. He dug his toe into the eave of the roof. Summoning all his strength, he pushed down on his injured palm, and with the help of his foot pulling on the eave he began to push himself back up to safety. He was almost there when the eave bent and cracked loudly, and with a final

116

surge he thrust himself back onto the roof. He rolled to the center and lay there, catching his breath.

Perhaps five minutes passed. Maybe more, maybe less. He lay in the rain cursing himself for the whole damn waste of it all. He hadn't learned a goddamn thing. All he'd gotten for nearly losing his life was a cut palm.

He raised his hand close to his eyes and examined it. The cut wasn't even serious. It would heal by morning. He held the cut out for the rain to wash but the rain stopped.

He almost laughed.

He crawled to his feet, his soaked clothing hanging heavily from his body. He stared into the wind and thought about the long trip back over the cars. The wind had become warm and would quickly dry the roofs. It might even dry his clothing. But for some reason he didn't feel like going back the way he'd come. He would pass over the party in the saloon car, then drop down and go inside.

He was about to move when a shot was fired in the caboose. Shaking his head, he reluctantly got down and began to once again lower himself to look through the window. He took his original position—without the rain it seemed a hell of a lot safer—and looked to see what the shooting was all about. Even as he looked, a second shot was fired.

Cranshaw was shooting at the wall. He held a fresh bottle. He waved his gun and fired a shot through the ceiling.

Moy didn't appear to be disturbed. He said something which caused Cranshaw to holster his gun. Hip Sing proceeded to clear the paraphernalia from the top of the trunk and opened the lid.

Amazement crossed the features of Marquez and Cranshaw when they saw the contents of the trunk: bricks wrapped in greased paper.

Moy rose from his chair. He picked up a brick, brought it to his lips and kissed it. He grinned. The grin spread into a laugh as he unwrapped the brick. Slocum didn't have to hear to know the high-crazed pitch of the laughter. Moy threw aside the wrapping and held out the brick. He put an arm around Hip Sing; the two of them shook with laughter. Marquez and Cranshaw stared at the brick and between them passed a look of obvious greed. The brick was the same gray substance Moy was smoking.

The Commissioner was alone at the dining car table where Slocum had left him. Asleep, his head pillowed in his arms, he snored like a steam-powered rasp. Slocum grabbed his shoulder and pulled him awake.

"I told you to stay with the madame."

"Next time tell 'er." The Commissioner rubbed his bloodshot eyes with trembling hands. He was deathly pale, and he smelled. There was a vomit stain on his vest. "She finished eatin' an' went off on 'er own."

"You all right?" Slocum asked with concern.

"Course I'm all righ'." He threw out his arms in a gesture of impatience. "Been waitin' on you! Waitin' to help." He leaned forward and looked Slocum up and down. "You been fuckin' that seal? You're all wet."

"You've puked on yourself."

"Never could stand a seal fucker. Queer fellers, seal fuckers. Met one once in—"

"Commissioner, you've been sick."

The Commissioner noticed the stain on his vest and frowned. He thumped his chest and hacked gruffly, "Summer cold, summer cold. Gimme a minute to clean up. I'll come help." He picked up a glass and splashed water over his vest, then awkwardly wiped at the stain with a napkin.

"Help with what?" Slocum asked.

"Makin' nightly rounds, ain't you? Think I'm a-goin' to let you walk alone?"

"Tonight's taken care of," Slocum said. The Commissioner's pale face was suddenly, sadly broken. Slocum

118

added, "I'd appreciate you being with me tomorrow, though."

The Commissioner brightened, obviously pleased. "Shouldn't have gone without me, stranger."

Slocum hooked a grin. "Why do you insist on calling me stranger?"

"Sounds more honest 'n Green." The Commissioner started to lift himself from his chair, but his weight was too much for him. He sighed and sank back down. "She shuts me up by clappin' her hands, you go off on your own. Know what she talks 'bout while you're gone? Ice! We're a-travelin' east at an unholy speed, and she's worryin' over ice."

Slocum extended a hand. "Take hold. I'll help you to your quarters."

The Commissioner hit out at Slocum's hand. "Don't need no help."

Slocum raised his hands in a gesture of surrender. "You win."

"Bein' sick an' a little drunk don' make me dead. Not yet it don't!"

"Meant no offense, Commissioner."

"First you wake me up, then you want to put me to bed." Color had begun to enter the man's features. "Whyn't you leave me be if you don't want my help. I ain't no senile wreck. I know what's a-goin' on. Goddamn dragon's draggin' you all straight to hell!"

"Just how much do you know?" Slocum asked.

"Her reasons for Wisconsin. Diggin' up a man out o' the past jus' to kill him. Pure crazy. She's goin' backwards. Si' down, stranger."

Slocum remained standing.

"Person doesn't get ahead goin' backwards."

"Depends on what's chasing a person," said Slocum.

"You sound crazy as her. Don' 'spect you'd want to walk back to the saloon? Or maybe find a waiter to get us a bottle. You could catch your death in them wet clothes."

119

"Waiters have all gone to bed, Commissioner."

" 'Fraid you'd say that." The Commissioner winked and tapped the side of his head with a bent finger. "I know where the fun is."

Slocum was convinced the Commissioner had nothing to say, but a new thought occurred to him. "How much is opium selling for on the illegal market?"

"Why should I know?"

"You were in Frisco politics."

The Commissioner fumbled in a pocket until he found a single cigar and box of matches. He struck a match and lit up. His hands still shook and he didn't look well, but a wary amusement had entered his eyes and his veined nose had begun to blossom. "So you found out 'bout Moy's trunk." He pulled on the cigar to get it going. "Told you I use to give the Chinese people jobs. Terrible gossips, them Chinese. Rumor the last few weeks was that Moy was buyin' up all the opium in Califor—"

"Why the hell didn't you tell me?"

The Commissioner absently rubbed the wet stain on his vest. He pointed to a chair and waited for Slocum to sit down before speaking. "I'm on your side, stranger. Make no mistake 'bout that. Yours an' hers." Again he tapped a bent finger against his head. "Fun. Up here's 'bout the only place I get to take my fun. A goodly share o' the fun o' this trip is watchin' all of you work out your mandarin plots. Be robbin' myself of pleasure if I wasn't to let you find things out for yourself."

Slocum worked to control his rising anger. "I'm not traveling east for fun, Commissioner. This is no game."

"Oh, it is to me. A fine game."

"Someone broke into Madame Lu's private car tonight. They could have been waiting there to kill her."

"Not her. You maybe. Moy don't want her dead just yet. They ransack the place?"

"It was all very neat. Came in through a window, went out the same way."

"Marquez," nodded the Commissioner. "Cranshaw's

120

too big to squeeze in a train window. Moy wouldn't risk himself or Hip Sing. How'd you spot it?"

"Marquez pried a knife under the window sash to slip the bolt. He put a scratch in the wood. I might have shrugged off just the scratch, but when Marquez left, he tied a waxed string in a slip knot and pulled the bolt lock behind him. Flecks of wax fell off the string."

"Goddamn, if you ain't an observin' cuss." The Commissioner nodded his head with approval. "What was it all for?"

"I don't know. I figure it won't happen again. Marquez either found what he was looking for, or he knows it isn't there. Why do you say Moy doesn't want Madame Lu dead?"

The cigar shot out of the Commissioner's mouth as he went into a fit of coughing. He doubled over with loud, wracking coughs, and his hand scratched over the tabletop until he found a napkin. He coughed into the napkin for a full minute.

"Damned if I don't sound like Doc Holliday." The Commissioner's cigar had burned a small circle into the tablecloth. He laughed weakly and shoved the cigar back into his mouth. "You plan on tellin' her 'bout the break-in?"

"No reason."

"Sort o' what I reckoned." The Commissioner twisted a finger against his head. "The all of you play your games. You tell her 'bout the break-in, she maybe tells you what it was done for. Means also she's been keepin' things 'from you. You don't tell her, well good hell, you'll know somethin' she don't."

The man went into another brief spasm of coughing. "You maybe don't like my game. But I play it fair. Here's the rules. Ask me anything you want. If I know a answer I'll tell it."

Slocum slammed a fist into the table. "You're like a goddamn kid."

"I'm in a 'nique position to have things my way."

"I could throw you off the train."

121

"Yep. I'd be dead first bounce. All I'd lose is a couple months. You'd lose what I can tell you."

The Commissioner was pulling the strings. Old and sick, a cantankerous bastard, stubborn, no doubt more full of crap than a honey bucket, but he pulled the strings. Threats wouldn't frighten him; no argument would ever shake loose his foolish notion of a game.

"Why does Moy want the madame alive?" Slocum asked.

"Money. She sunk near all she owns in this here train. You're ridin' on over a million dollars. Course she always makes a profit. When she turns the legal title over to the man from Barnum, he'll hand her cash. Moy wants her safe 'n sound 'til she's got that cash."

"Then the break-in was to find the title?"

"Reckon so," nodded the Commissioner. "The title an' her will. See, Moy's got no real proof he's her next o' kin. All the family documents got lost back in China. And the madame's will. It leaves everything to charity. I know 'bout the will 'cause I drew it up. Moy knows about it, too. The madame had him sign it as a witness."

"Are the title and the will on this train?"

The Commissioner shook his head. "Mailed ahead. Locked up in a Chicago vault."

"What's the opium for?"

"I reckon Moy plans on selling it in Chicago. Use the money to hire an army and take over. Those clowns he hired to get you, they're no doubt workin' on his promise of a share."

Slocum remembered the look of greed Marquez and Cranshaw had exchanged when they saw the trunk of opium. "Maybe those clowns will take care of Moy for me."

The Commissioner laughed. "That's the idea Moy wants you to have. Don't know how you learned about the trunk, but one way or 'nother, Moy would've made sure you found out. Why the hell you think that trunk weren't loaded 'til you happened along? You were 'sposed to see it, 'spose to get curious. Just like you were supposed to get the notion Cranshaw and Marquez would kill Moy to steal the dope. Every false notion Moy can feed you makes you a little more off guard."

"Does she know about the opium?"

"I 'magine she heard the same gossip I heard. Reckon she refuses to believe it."

Slocum ruefully shook his head. "Chinese pride?"

"Hell of a thing to understand, ain't it?"

13

The lamps in the private car had been adjusted to low blue flames, no brighter than candles. The curtains were drawn around the four-poster bed. Han Su called from behind the curtains as he entered, "Is that you, John Slocum?"

Slocum mumbled a response and quickly undressed. He went to a sideboard where there was a basin, a pitcher of water, soap and towels. While washing himself, he thought about the things the Commissioner had said. And about the unspoken things the man had implied.

"My bed feels empty without you, John Slocum. Please hurry."

He threw aside a towel and caught a glimpse of himself in a mirror. His muscular body was streaked with black and blue marks. He moved to the liquor cabinet and took out a bottle of sour mash. A low, catlike murmur came from the curtained bed. He poured two fingers of whiskey into a glass and turned to look at the bed. The murmur came from behind the curtains again.

"I've some thinking to do," Slocum said.

"Cannot your thoughts wait until morning?"

"I've just had a long talk with the Commissioner."

She opened the curtains. A sheet was pulled to her neck. A white rose was in her dark hair, and beneath the sheet he saw the soft contours of her body.

"The Commissioner is a provocateur, John Slocum."

123

He sipped his drink and watched as she brought a hand from under the sheet and patted the empty side of the bed. He glanced at the bed and said, "Why don't you tell cousin Moy certain papers are already in Chicago? Why didn't you tell me about the papers?"

A sly pout creased her lips. "Moy would not believe the simple truth. And of what value is such information to you? My papers are of a business nature. Did I not say you were not to bother yourself about the business."

"Once you sell your train you won't need me. You'll be able to buy the whole U.S. Cavalry to do your protecting. And to sack your town."

Her almond eyes were suddenly moist. "Your tone of mistrust hurts me. Perhaps you wish to revenge yourself for my tone to you at dinner. I must apologize. My head was weak from too much wine, and I was much confused. The girls' gift of a quilt had deeply touched me."

"I wonder if anything really touches you, Han Su."

She threw back the sheet. She was naked but for stockings and garters. The black silk stockings were a thin mesh that wrapped her legs with the intricate patterns of a spider's web. Her legs were slightly parted. The soft blue light flickered across her bronze skin.

"Come, John Slocum."

He put down his drink and went to the bed. He stood above her, watching, and her every breath created the slow rise and fall of a pale fire. The gentle slope of her breasts, her flat belly, the flow of her hips were a liquid gold. She moved. The white rose fell from her hair to a pillow.

She reached for him and moved a hand along his thigh. She put her lips against his thigh, cradled his balls in her palm, and moved her lips to the head of his cock.

She whispered, "Do I no longer excite you?"

She lifted her rose from the pillow and brushed its petals across his cock. She brought the rose to her lips and tore a single petal with her teeth. She put out her tongue, the white petal at the tip of it, and as she moved over her breasts, she very slowly curled her tongue into her mouth to swallow the petal. She teased her nipples into firm points with the rose's stem and traced the flower down her belly and across her mound of curls, down past the dark band of a garter. A sharp, high cry escaped her lips, and her eyes widened as she twisted the stem into the silken mesh of a stocking and pierced her flesh with a thorn. A red line bled into the black lace and she moved the garter to hold the thorn in place.

"You fought hard today, John Slocum. It is right I should bleed and feel a bit of your pain."

She wrapped her arms around his legs and took his cock into her mouth, swallowing the whole of him. He watched the sleek flow of her hair as she sucked, watched the liquid flow of her body, the golden skin, the rose trapped in the spider mesh of silk. A tremble coursed through him. He pushed her from him. She fell back on the bed, her legs open to receive him, her body an amber cascade of flame.

She cried out as he dropped over her, her hips rushing to meet him, thrusting to meet his thrust. But he didn't enter her. He held himself above her, his weight taken by his elbows, and cupped her breasts with his hands. Her breath came quickly; she sighed and twisted to reach his cock with her cunt, her hair whipping the pillow. She called to him. There was urgency in her call, also demand, and he tantalizingly slid his cock along the line of her cunt, refusing to give in to her demand. To-night he would take her when he was ready, when he had pulled her all the way to the edge, that high edge she had never allowed.

He moved his tongue down her belly and licked the small round circle of her navel. Her hips thrashed as he went lower. He held her hips tight to the bed and buried his head between her legs and bit her thigh, biting with an increasing pressure until she began to moan, a low steady moaning, and he put his tongue to her cunt. He licked the fold of her, pushing his tongue deep. Her moans became high and intense. His tongue moved up the fold of her cunt; he caught her button between his lips and stabbed it with his tongue. Her hands grasped his shoulders; her nails dug into him. She was almost to the edge, but one part of her fought him. She dug her nails into his flesh trying to push him away, push his stabbing tongue from her button, yet at the same time her hips thrust her cunt hard to him. He moved a hand along the taut cheeks of her ass and found the tight bud of her asshole. He pushed a finger against the bud while still licking her and she thrust to escape his finger. *"No,"* she cried as his finger entered her ass, and then, *"yes,"* and she started over the edge, calling his name and *"yes, yes, yes."*

He moved on top of her, tearing the white rose from her stocking. As he plunged into her he crushed the flower against her breasts with his weight and rode her to a quick, wrenching climax.

14

They pulled into their first stop shortly after dawn, and before noon the dragon was open for business. It was a small community—the Commissioner said living here would be about as exciting as watching mushrooms grow—but news of their coming had preceded them and they didn't lack for customers. The saloon was full; the gambling cars were busy. A growing line of men waited outside the cars where the girls were working. Trixie's Gleason splashed in a tub near the head of the line.

The Commissioner laughed, "Damned if that seal don't look like it's takin tickets."

Slocum grinned. "Judging by the length of that line of customers, maybe we should put it to business."

"Speakin' o' business," the Commissioner asked, "why you 'spose the madame went off 'stead of bein' here for her opening?"

Slocum hadn't seen Han Su since breakfast. She had

chattered so much about how good she was feeling that when she left with the Commissioner, Slocum was frankly relieved to be free of her. He'd sat and enjoyed a quiet second cup of coffee, then involved himself with sorting out some of the hundred-odd little problems that cropped up with the opening.

"I thought she went with you to see the sheriff?" Slocum asked.

"We saw him. Saw the judge an' mayor, too. Gave all three an envelope. Next thing I know, she's ridin' off with three cowboys. Christ in hell if she weren't actin' like a schoolgirl the whole time with me."

Before Slocum could pursue the subject, a man stepped from the line and approached them. He removed a weathered straw hat, shuffled his feet, and scratched all over. "You, eh, men. You look to be—" He rubbed a finger at an eye and found himself a bit of grit. "You look to have somethin' to do with this, eh, this here locomotive."

"We're with it," said the Commissioner.

"Think maybe something could be done to speed things up. See, lot of us boys waitin' here, we—" He twisted his hat, nodded, scratched again, nodded. "We got us certain responsibilities. Wives an' farms to tend. I'm not rightly sure how to state this but—"

"I understand," said Slocum, "but our girls believe in giving a man a good time for his money."

"Now I'm surely in favor of that. Yes, sir. And none of us objects to paying for what's good. No, sir. But standin' here, it puts us right smack in the open. A man's wife, well, you know how curious a woman can get. A locomotive like this is sort of an attraction."

Slocum thought over the situation. "What if we give you men numbers? You can wait in the saloon or casino cars until we call your number."

"I'm not real sure you understand our predicament. The most of us, well, we're right religious. We don't hold with gambling or drinking."

Moy appeared from around the edge of the crowd.

Marquez and Cranshaw were with him. He must have been close enough to hear the conversation because he went to the man and after a stately bow said, "Your problem, sir, I have seen to. The line shall move more smoothly now."

Moy was dressed all in red silk today, and his pigtail flashed from the sunlight. The man's mouth fell open; he damn near dropped his hat as he looked Moy up and down.

Moy paid no attention to the farmer's gaping. "Please partake of the company of my quarters until your wait is ended. I reside at the end of the train. My man, Hip Sing, waits there to serve you light refreshment."

The man had to swallow a few times before managing to speak. "That's most accommodating. Yes, sir." He then walked toward the caboose.

Moy turned to Slocum and the Commissioner. "May all the problems of our long journey be so easily resolved."

The Commissioner responded, "Mighty big gesture, Moy, openin' your quarters."

"My quarters are always open to all. Indeed, there was a moment last night, Mr. Green, when I thought you had chosen to call on us in roundabout fashion. I heard a sound upon the roof. It was, of course, but the noise of a rain shower."

"If I decide to pay a call, I'll come through the front door." Slocum glanced at Marquez. "Like a gentleman."

Marquez's lips twisted into an ugly slash. Cranshaw uttered an ugly grunt.

"You sound like a rutting pig, Cranshaw," said Slocum.

Cranshaw rested his hands against the butts of his holstered guns. "I'm not so easy as that dummy you beat up, Green."

"You try to pull those guns," said Slocum, "and I'll kick you in the balls so fast you'll shoot your toes off."

"Gentlemen," said Moy. "Is this my ignorance of Western culture or are these words of hostility I hear?"

128

"What did you mean, Moy, by telling the dude the line would move more smoothly?" Slocum turned toward Moy.

"A whore is a venal creature, Mr. Green. She would prolong a man's pleasure in hopes of receiving an extra sum of money, a tip for herself. It is to the best interests of the dragon that I have destroyed such venality."

"Just how did you do that?"

A smile creased Moy's thin mouth. "A simple threat. Spoken while Senor Marquez was somewhat crudely paring his nails with one of his silver-handled daggers."

"You threatened to cut 'em," muttered the Commissioner glumly.

"One does not threaten what one would not do. At so early a juncture in our journey, I would not consider damaging our merchandise. After all, do we not travel with but a minimal number of whores? Such drastic measures may become necessary in the future, however."

"You don't lay a hand on any of them, Moy," Slocum said coolly.

"I shall do whatever has to be done. As for today, I threatened none of them. It seems the sentimental creatures have formed an attachment to a dog and a stupid seal. The seal, naturally, will not survive the hot crossings, but this they are too foolish to realize. They work quickly now. Every trick, every orifice of their vile bodies works to render men limp and useless. They do this because they fear for their animals."

Slocum wanted to talk with Mr. Peasly. The Commissioner tagged along, steadily muttering his hatred for Moy.

"Crazy sonofabitch. Threatenin' to kill a seal."

"The madame wouldn't stand for it," Slocum replied.

"She might not like it, but she'd let him do it. There's stories 'bout how he kept discipline back in the Palace. Near horsewhipped a girl to death once. 'Nother time there was a lovely figured woman he didn't want to damage. They tied her down. His toady, Hip Sing, used red hot needles under her tits and on her cunt."

"I wouldn't stand for that."

"Stranger, you're assumin' you'll be around to stop him."

Mr. Peasly was moving along the outside of his engine with an oilcan and rag. He greeted Slocum and the Commissioner with a cheerful but weary wave. Lines of exhaustion showed through his soot-streaked features.

"Ain't you slept none?" asked the Commissioner.

"Mr. Green, tell the portly man for me that you always tend to your horse 'fore beddin' down your own self."

"True," said Slocum. "But you've a couple helpers to grease your gears."

"Hell, this ain't no gear I'm tendin'," laughed Mr. Peasly. "How you like your ride so far?"

"Been seasick all mornin'," answered the Commissioner with a sigh.

Mr. Peasly shook his rag in the Commissioner's face. "Wipe the shit outta your brain, you old fart. My train rides smoother 'n a barge on still water. Never pushed 'er 'bove forty mile an hour last night. Had a couple stretches where I wanted to."

The Commissioner gasped, "Forty mile an—!"

"When we hit them long flat stretches you hold your nuts and keep a fast one. I may push this lady over a hundred."

"You can get that speed?" asked Slocum.

"I got steam pushin' me, Mr. Green. Pushing the finest engine ever built. I'd say a hundred is conser'tive. If I choose not to use all my steam, it'll be 'cause of that damn tail sticking up in the air."

"We rounded a hairpin curve last night. If you had been going five miles faster, what would have happened then?"

"If I'd been going *one* mile faster, the tail would've gone over."

"Take the whole train with it?"

"Not likely." Mr. Peasly rubbed his chin and a cagey, conspiratorial edge entered his voice. "Remember that Twinkle Toes the madame had design this train? He was always so damn busy making things look pretty, well, he didn't notice me changin' a couple of his specifications. That caboose is held by a slender, hollow rod. I saw to its installation myself. If the tail fails, well, that rod will snap clean as a twig. I had to do it, had to protect my train."

"I think you did right, Mr. Peasly," said Slocum.

"Damn right!" added the Commissioner.

"What's more," continued Slocum, "I think that tail's a piece of shit. We just may have to do something about it."

A clattering filled the air as three covered freight wagons pulled up to the train. Han Su rode with the driver of the first wagon. She stood up before the horses had been reined to a full halt and eagerly yelled to Slocum.

Slocum went to her. He opened his arms to help her down from the wagon, but she ignored his reach. With a playful shout she leaped from the wagon seat and caught her arms around his neck. She hung from him, her feet not touching the ground, and hugged him and whispered a funny little intimacy in his ear before releasing her hold. She opened her arms wide and spun herself round and round, laughing, her laughter free and light as the song of a bird.

"I have found ice!"

"Found what?" said Slocum.

"A whole barn full of ice packed in sawdust. It was cut from a nearby lake the past winter."

"You bought a barn of ice—?"

"But of course. The man would not give it to me."

"—just to chill your wine?"

131

"Not wine. For the seal for when we cross the desert."

Han Su ran along the train. She rapped on all the windows, giving no heed to the business doings she interrupted, and shouted out the news of ice.

15

At sunset they put up what looked like a very high clothesline and hung several lanterns from it. A breeze stirred the lanterns, and in the darkness the swinging lanterns sent odd patterns twisting along the ground and over the growing crowd outside the train.

Business had been steady through the day. It picked up considerably with the darkness. By ten o'clock it was clear the dragon wasn't equipped to keep pace with the crowd's demands. A man generally paid two-bits for a shot of whiskey in this community, and though the saloon was jammed wall-to-wall, none of the men were happy about shelling out two dollars a drink. They paid it, though, figuring their turn at a girl would soon come. But there were only forty girls and a man could nurse a drink just so long.

Outside, a line of some fifty men waited to get to the girls. For some it was their second or third wait. Complaints were heard about the price of twenty dollars a throw. They pushed one another and argued over their place in line. A few fights broke out. One fight became so rowdy it threatened to involve the whole line. Slocum broke up the fight and told the men in line he would close down the train if they didn't settle down.

He and the Commissioner pushed through the casino cars checking on the dealers. The cars were hot and smokey and so jammed they couldn't get near many tables. Most of the players were also waiting for a girl. More grumbling could be heard over the twenty-dollar price.

Slocum and the Commissioner slipped off the train

for a smoke and a little quiet. They walked on the dark side away from the action, smoking and talking.

They came upon Trixie, unintentionally frightening her. She quickly threw down a cigaret and started for the train. Nervously she said, "Just answering a call of nature. Going right back to—"

Slocum stopped her by placing a hand on her shoulder. She was trembling.

"Relax," he said.

"Moy says we're to keep working steady."

"Take yourself a few minutes' break," said Slocum.

The Commissioner pushed a cigar at her. "Smoke one o' these 'stead of them loose roll-your-owns."

She glanced in the direction of the caboose. "If you men say it's okay—" She accepted the cigar, and the Commissioner lit it for her.

"How are the girls holding up?" asked Slocum.

"We girls hold up to what we fucking well have to. Only Moy's got us popping the customers' nuts 'fore they even get their britches off."

Slocum smiled around his cigar. Whenever he was near Trixie, he was reminded of the Little Bo Beep costume she had been wearing the first time he saw her. He'd never quite matched up that original image with her blunt language.

"These men want to feel some pussy for their money," she said. "They ain't going to put up much longer for this in, out and all over shit. They ain't polite Frisco dandies."

"Don't you worry none," said the Commissioner. "Me an' the stranger'll handle any problem."

Trixie looked at Slocum. "You think my seal's safe?"

"Safe as royalty," laughed Slocum. "Asleep on a block of ice in his own private boxcar."

"Where's the dog?" asked the Commissioner.

"We girls got him. One of us was thinking of putting him in an act." She uttered a short, brittle laugh. "Don't look like Moy'll be giving us time to do the training."

A shot rang out from the other side of the train.

Slocum spat out his cigar. He loosened his gun in its holster and ran toward the train.

The crowd was shouting, and he heard a series of sharp cracks that sounded like fireworks. He leaped between two cars, coming out facing the crowd. His sudden appearance startled and silenced a cursing mule skinner. The man was waving a gun, and his other hand cracked an evil black bullwhip. The crowd was cheering the mule skinner. He must have fired into the air because no body lay on the ground. He stood beneath the lanterns. With his burly features dripping angry sweat and his shirt tail swinging loose around his waist, he cast a wide, grotesque shadow.

Slocum quietly said, "Holster that gun, friend. And coil your whip."

The mule skinner cracked his whip. A spray of dirt bounced off Slocum's boots. The crowd, drunk now and almost as disorderly as a mob, roared.

"I been cheated," shouted the mule skinner. He snapped up his whip and took a step toward Slocum. "I want my money back."

"Whoa there, friend. I recognize your face. You've climbed in with a girl two, three times already. You got no complaint."

"Three times! I want my sixty dollars."

Similar complaints were shouted from the crowd. It began to edge in nearer to Slocum and the mule skinner.

Slocum said, "Friend, if you can't control yourself—"

"Been fuckin' all my life. Ain't been milked so fast since I was twelve an' diddled my daddy's cow."

Slocum smiled broadly. "I see I'm not dealing with no dude. Put away your gun. Come along with me."

By now the Commissioner had caught up with Slocum. The mule skinner cocked his head and looked at them suspiciously.

"Give a listen, friend." Slocum lowered his voice, and the mule skinner had to move closer to hear him. "We might cheat some dumb dude but never a man like yourself."

"Come along," said the Commissioner. "We'll give you your money."

The mule skinner rubbed the barrel of his gun over his sweaty cheeks. "You men dealin' straight?"

The Commissioner winked. "We'll even throw in a little somethin' extra. Ever seen two women together?"

The mule skinner holstered his gun and coiled his whip. They led him away from the crowd. When they reached the dark shadows, Slocum maneuvered the mule skinner between himself and the Commissioner. He looked over his shoulder to be sure no one had followed, pulled his gun and knocked the mule skinner unconscious. The Commissioner caught the man as he dropped.

"Let him fall," Slocum ordered. "Find Mr. Peasly and tell him to fire up his engine. Then go to the madame's car. Keep her there. Tie her down if you have to, but keep her there. Don't open her door to anyone but me."

"Want for Mr. Peasly to pull out soon's he gets a head of steam?"

"This train moves at the next sign of trouble. I don't care if he has to get out and push it."

"What about them customers on board?"

"We'll drop them down the road. Now move!"

Slocum hurried back to where the crowd had become a shoving, faceless mass. They had whiskey now. Bottles were being passed around and grabbed and fought over. The swinging lanterns madly distorted their furious struggles. Marquez and Cranshaw were selling the whiskey across a makeshift bar—which consisted of a plank and two barrels. Moy, partially concealed by shadow, stood on the walkway of a car.

Slocum approached Moy. "Selling whiskey to these men your idea?"

Moy stepped farther into shadow. The length of his pigtail gleamed dully. "The customers could not get to the whiskey, so the whiskey came to the customers."

135

"Selling them whiskey's like feeding wind to a tornado."

"The business of business is profit," responded Moy. "There is much profit in whiskey, as it causes a man's pockets to feel heavy even as he lightens them."

"Forget your goddamn flowery language. We're facing a riot."

Slocum went to the bar. Men pressed against the bar demanding whiskey. They clumsily pushed forward, and when their mass threatened to topple the plank, Cranshaw rudely shoved them back. Six open cases stood between Cranshaw and Marquez, four of them still full.

Marquez glanced at Slocum. His eyes were alert and darting, taking in every shifting movement of the crowd. A wan smile crossed his lips. "It appears, *senor,* we are temporarily on the same side."

"Give them the whiskey!" exclaimed Slocum.

"Fuckin' farmers don' wanta pay," muttered Cranshaw.

"Moy wants fifty dollars a bottle," explained Marquez. "It is rather like waving a red flag before the bull."

Slocum cursed out Moy and said, "Fire over their heads if they riot."

"Over their heads, into their heads. *Senor,* we do not have the bullets to stop them."

"Fire high and get into the train. Mr. Peasly will move at the sound of a shot."

"If he has enough steam to pull the train," said Marquez. "In any case, *senor,* it's better for men such as ourselves to die together than to kill one another."

A man plunged down across the plank, desperately trying to reach a bottle. Cranshaw delivered a powerhouse blow that lifted the man back into the crowd.

That does it, thought Slocum.

He grabbed three bottles and jumped onto the plank. He swung one of the bottles above his head. The mob shifted and swayed as all eyes followed the swinging bottle. He threw it high into the darkness above the line

136

of lanterns. A wild cheer erupted when the bottle dropped back into the light, and the mob lunged to catch it.

Slocum threw the other two bottle in different directions, far over the mob. The crowd lunged backward, separating into two groups trying to get the bottles. Slocum drew his gun and shouted, "Celebrate, boys! Free drinks!" He fired a shot at the sky and jumped down from the plank.

Cranshaw and Marquez began throwing bottles. They spaced their throws, separating the men into smaller groups that fought amongst themselves for the catch.

"Force them back as far as possible," said Slocum. "When you throw out all your whiskey, get aboard."

Mr. Peasly had to have heard Slocum's shot. Slocum looked at the silver sheen of the unmoving wheels.

Moy suddenly charged down from the train. He screamed at his henchmen to stop throwing away the whiskey and ran toward Slocum. "Stop this! You cannot give away my whiskey!"

Two men broke from the crowd and stopped Moy before he could reach Slocum. The men were crazy drunk. Moy tried to skirt around them, but they moved to block his way.

"You will please step aside," Moy said coolly.

The two men roared. One slapped his leg. "Is it a boy or girl!"

"Looks a girl," said the other. "Only girls run with their arms coverin' their chests. Protects their tits!"

"Do not insult me," said Moy. Arms across his chest, head dipped, he looked menacingly up through his lashes at them.

"Insult you, sweetie! Hell, I'm goin' to fuck you."

The other man laughed, "What if she turns out to be a boy?"

"I'll cut off his girl's haircut."

The man reached for Moy. There was a lightning quick movement as Moy twisted his head and his pigtail lashed like a whip into the man's face. The man

137

screeched and tried to raise his hands to his cut face. Moy pulled a cleaver from a sleeve and smashed the blade into the man's skull.

The second man was too stunned to react, as his friend slowly crumpled to the ground. Only when Moy stooped to retrieve his cleaver did the second man move. He reached for a gun. He was slow, however, and Slocum easily outdrew him. But before Slocum could shoot, the man screamed and fell backward, clutching at his chest, vainly trying to grasp the slim, silver-handled dagger that had killed him.

The mob pitched forward. Slocum stopped it by firing two shots in the air.

"*Senor!* The train."

Marquez and Cranshaw were firing as they backed toward the train. The damn wheels still weren't turning.

Slocum faced the mob. *Was Peasly deaf?* He had three shots left. He wasn't going to waste them shooting at air. The mob was massing to charge again, but if they did, three of them would never reach him.

"*Senor,* quick!"

Slocum turned to see Cranshaw taking aim with his pistol at something above Slocum's head. Then, out of the corner of his eye, Slocum saw a silver glint of movement. The wheels were beginning to move. At that moment the mob charged.

Cranshaw fired. His bullet sliced through the line holding the lanterns. Slocum was standing directly beneath them. He sprang backward, the lanterns smashing into a stream of flames only inches away from his feet. A pool of fire splashed his trouser legs. He rolled to the ground and slapped out his burning trousers.

The mob couldn't break through the streaming flames. Some men fired wildly at the moving train; others threw rocks. One of the mob had been splashed with flame, and he ran about screaming and making himself a human torch.

Slocum rushed to the train. He grabbed hold and

138

pulled himself aboard. He found himself sharing one of the small walkways with Marquez.

"For a moment, *senor,* I thought we were going to lose you."

"I'd have been caught under those lanterns if you hadn't called when you did." Slocum held out his hand.

Marquez smiled and refused to shake hands. *"Senor, only temporarily were we on the same side."*

16

Moy laid low for the next three weeks. Once a day the Commissioner and Slocum would go with Madame Lu to the caboose. The two men would wait while she and Moy went over the books of the past day's business. The lid of Moy's steamer trunk served as a desk top. Han Su and Moy spoke Chinese to each other, so there was no telling what passed between them. He would lay out the cash while she made calculations with an abacus.

Cranshaw and Marquez always sat at the opposite end of the car from Slocum and the Commissioner, Cranshaw staring like a hungry ferret at the cash being counted. Marquez usually kept his attention on the chessboard. Once he gestured an invitation for Slocum to join him in a game.

When Han Su and Moy had finished their business, she would bag most of the cash and leave Moy only a little money to work with. Hip Sing always squatted cross-legged near Moy; just about the time when Han Su would bag the money, Hip Sing would utter a girlish keen and cover his eyes like a see-no-evil monkey.

Together Slocum and Han Su always locked the cash in the safe in her car. Sometimes she told Slocum what she and Moy had discussed, but it was always unimportant things. One afternoon, Slocum said, "I'm not interested in business trivia."

"But do you not wish to know how we prosper?"

"I know how we're doing by the size of those bags. I'm not concerned about how much a particular girl brings in on a certain night."

"Such is not a trivial concern. It allows us to know how hard the girls do their job."

Slocum grinned. "I imagine cousin Moy isn't too happy they're all working well."

"Keeping our business a smoothly flowing thing requires many elements, John Slocum. The fear the girls feel for Moy is one element. Another is the trust they have in myself. Still another is yourself. The girls have come to look upon you as a symbol of strength. They feel that with you on hand they are secure."

Slocum stretched his arms and effected a yawn. "Shucks, madame. I'm just a humble big brother."

Han Su grinned. "I confess, were their interest in you not beneficial to the dragon's success, I would feel jealousy."

Slocum pulled her close and kissed her.

"John Slocum!" she giggled with mock alarm, "is this a symbol of strength I feel against my thigh?"

"Why do you make everything so goddamn complex, lady? This is a simple hard cock rubbing against your thigh."

She broke from him and quickly removed her clothes. "Please, come simply fuck me."

The dragon crossed into Nevada on the twenty-third night. It was a hot, full-moon night. Slocum and the Commissioner were making rounds when Mr. Peasly announced the crossing by blowing the dragon's whistle. They were on a walkway when the whistle screeched. The train was moving at a fast speed, but even at a crawl the Commissioner was never agile in stepping between cars, and the sudden screech startled him and caused him to slip. Though he was holding onto a safety strap, as he started to fall he twisted awkwardly and

140

one of his feet kicked off the walkway. Slocum hurriedly grabbed the man's leg and pulled it back to safety.

"Damn! A man could lose a foot that way," the Commissioner gasped as they moved into the next car. He gripped the back of a seat in the car to steady himself.

"Sure as hell pinched your toes a bit," Slocum said.

"Damn gout does that already." The Commissioner was panting from his brief exertion. "Why in hell does Mr. Peasly got to blow his horn all a-time an' travel at the devil's pace?"

Slocum gently pushed the man into the seat. "Let's relax a minute."

"Got our rounds," protested the Commissioner.

"They'll keep a minute."

A light thump hit the roof. Slocum tensed and waited for another sound. None came.

The Commissioner opened a window. Wind ruffled his muttonchops as he leaned over, cleared his throat and spat.

Slocum remained curious about the sound on the roof.

"Might o' been fittin' if I smashed this gouty foot. Seein's how we just passed the first leg of the trip."

"Now comes the hard part," said Slocum.

"The hell you say."

"We've a dull landscape about two degrees hotter than hell to cross. I don't know how the girls will hold up."

"Looks right pretty in the moonlight. Anyways, none of 'em signed on for a vacation tour. They're here for the money. So long's Moy leaves well enough alone, no problems."

Slocum continued to think about the noise on the roof. "Moy's been doing what I told the madame to tell him to do. I think he's about to make a play."

The Commissioner pointed a finger at him. "Now

141

don't be takin' credit for the rules the madame installed after our near riot. Keepin' reg'lar business hours an' chargin' accordin' to what a community can pay is jus' common sense. You might've suggested it, but don't be so all fired certain she weren't all the time ahead o' you."

Slocum cocked his head, still listening.

Then he heard it. A footstep. A slow and unsteady footstep scraping across the roof. He leaned toward the window.

"Oh, I grant you," the Commissioner said, "she's been behavin' strange since you been around. Could all be play actin'. Fer instance, all her giggly ways with the seal. Buyin' it ice an' what-not. On a-surface it's kitten sweet o' her. But look how it's helpin' to keep the girls in line. Instead o' fussin' 'mongst themselves, they all together tend to them animals. Christ, Trixie's got the seal bouncin' a red rubber ball on its nose."

Slocum stared with disbelief out the window. He'd never known until now just how goddamn stupid Cranshaw truly was. Cranshaw was crouched on the roof above them. Crouched right out plain and letting the moon throw his shadow. The image was clear enough for Slocum to make out the shape of the gun Cranshaw held in his right hand.

Slocum put a finger to his lips. He pointed out the shadow to the Commissioner. He knew from his experience on the caboose that Cranshaw would have difficulty hearing a voice with the wind rushing in his ears. Nonetheless, he took no chances. "How fast you reckon we're going?" he whispered.

"Mr. Peasly said he could hit a hundred mile."

"Oh, I don't think we're anywhere near that speed. I suspect more like half that speed."

Slocum's eyes shifted to a cord running along the ceiling.

"Still a hell of a speed." The Commissioner followed Slocum's gaze. He laughed softly. "Man weren't meant
mn fast."

Slocum nodded agreement. He reached up and pulled the cord. The screech of the braking wheels covered any scream Cranshaw may have made as he plummeted off the train.

"Please stay in me." Han Su's voice was a soft and satisfied purr. Her arms and legs held Slocum tightly. "I love the feel of you inside me, John Slocum."

Slocum kissed the thin line of perspiration that had formed on her forehead when she climaxed. "Lady, you ought to know by now. This is just about my favorite position."

"But you have tasted your pleasure. It is uncommon for a man to stay in a woman once such has happened."

"I'm an uncommon man." Slocum smiled down at her. "As the Commissioner might say, this is a mere *coitus hiatus*."

"Never has it been this way for me. Always I have known how to please a man, never has a man—" Her face clouded for a moment and she bit her lip before saying, "After Wisconsin all my scars shall be healed. I am so looking forward to New York City."

Slocum pulled up, bracing himself on his hands, though he didn't pull out from her. "We're still in Utah. What's this about New York?"

"I am having the money from the sale of my dragon shipped to New York. From Wisconsin we shall go there and collect it."

It was too sudden, too out of nowhere for Slocum to swallow it. "Why?"

Han Su smiled. "Because I have never seen New York." She moved her hips against him and tried to pull him back into the embrace of her arms.

Slocum shot out a hand and pressed it to her forehead. "Why are you transferring your money? When did you decide this?"

Her eyes blinked with shock. "You are hurting me."

Slocum relaxed the pressure of his hand. "Answer me."

143

Her lips quivered. She looked about to weep. "Do you still mistrust me?"

"I'm trying not to."

"Until recently I had thought to convert my dragon money into arms and men to sack Peshtigo."

"Sacking a town!" Slocum's voice was thick with anger. "Senselessly killing innocent people. Marsden did that during the war. You knew I wouldn't stoop to that level. I made that clear from the beginning."

"Say no more! Please."

For the first time, Slocum saw fear in her. "You meant to double-cross me."

"Understand me!" Her head twisted and thrashed the pillow. Her eyes blinked to hold back her tears. "I have been driven by my desire, my need for revenge. I thought only of it. I yearn now for more. For a future. Our future."

She shook with fear. Desperation entered her voice, and her eyes were full and wet and Slocum didn't know how to read them. "There is a man in New York. In the Chinese quarter. He will guard my money and ask no questions of us. To carry the money to Wisconsin would be foolish. Marsden supplies Chicago with timber. Since we will be stopping their line of supply, it would be unwise to return to Chicago. Surely, John Slocum, surely you agree."

She trembled with such intensity that gooseflesh appeared on her skin. "With the combined monies of my train and Wisconsin, we shall be able to buy us an empire. Anywhere in the world. Just the two of us."

She weakly pulled at his shoulders with shaking hands. "John Slocum. Do you not know how much I love you?"

He looked into her wet, almond eyes. All he knew for sure was he wanted to believe. Slowly, almost reluctantly, he allowed her to pull him back into her embrace. Her nails gripped him as he covered her cool and trembling body, and her hips became a liquid magnet sucking him in.

144

* * *

On a bright and sunny afternoon the dragon pulled out in a rush from a siding near Ogden. The siding was not far from the Promontory site of the driving of the Golden Spike. The dragon's layover at the siding had been long and profitable, and Madame Lu wanted to stay there longer. Only one thing kept her from doing so: the news of a group of Mormon elders massing for a vigilante raid.

Slocum was just as happy to be on the road again. It was easier to keep an eye on things when the train was moving. Also, every mile crossed brought him a mile nearer to Marsden. Now that the long, bitter years of waiting to confront Marsden were coming to an end, Slocum found himself thinking more and more about the man. Dark and painful memories that time had somehow numbed were again sharp and vivid: the night of Marsden's Treachery, the shattering roar of cannon fire, the helpless cries of dying men. Most of all, Slocum remembered the vow he'd made, his vow to kill Marsden.

The man who had ridden to warn them of the vigilante raid had also delivered a telegram to Madame Lu. That evening Slocum sat in the casino, puffing a cigar, twisting the telegram into a tube between his palms. Outside, the last red rays of sunset burned the rocky landscape.

The Commissioner and the Ruby twins were laughing over a game of hearts at a nearby table. Trixie and another girl were teaching tricks to the animals. Other girls were sitting around gossiping. A few were sewing or writing letters.

Slocum smiled at the scene around him. It was all downright homey. And didn't at all match his thoughts. He sipped from his drink and unrolled the telegram to reread it.

The telegram was only five words long. "Peshtigo Indian waits in Omaha."

The train was crawling up a mountain. There had

been times lately when Slocum grew impatient if the train had to go slow. Tonight, though, he rather liked the slower pace. It matched his mood.

From the Indian, Slocum would learn what he needed to know to finalize his plans for Peshtigo. He had a rough plan sketched out in his mind. He wanted only two things from the Indian: the meat and the potatoes. Information on Marsden's security and a complete map of the Peshtigo area. Anything else the Indian offered would be gravy.

He listened to the rhythmic roll of the wheels. He leaned back in his seat and puffed his cigar. A smile of dark humor appeared on his face as he remembered a line expressing the way of his mood. Was it from Machiavelli? "Revenge is a dish best served cold."

He struck a match and lit the telegram. He dropped the flaming paper on the table and watched the bright flames burn it into a black, crumpled ball. The ball still smoldered as he put out his hand and crushed it into powder.

A red rubber ball bounced on the table. Its sudden, incongruous appearance caused him to laugh. He caught it and handed it back to Trixie.

"Sorry," she apologized. "We're teaching the little pissers a new trick."

Slocum brushed away the telegram's ashes. "What's the trick?"

"They almost got it learned. First the seal catches the ball on its nose. He spins it 'round some, then bats the fucker with his tail to the dog. Cute, huh?"

Slocum watched while Trixie went back to the animals. She got down on her knees, gave both the seal and the dog a kiss on the nose, then placed the ball on the tip of the seal's nose.

A Ruby twin said, "I sure ain't lookin' forward to Cheyenne."

"Be of good cheer," chuckled the Commissioner. "It's our last major layover."

"That true, Mr. Green?" a girl called to Slocum.

"It's the plan," he answered. "A few quick stops in Nebraska. Then straight through to Chicago."

The Ruby twin said, "They don't call Cheyenne 'Hell on Wheels' for nothing."

"Don't you worry none 'bout trouble," said the Commissioner. "You got the stranger an' me to take care o' you."

"Who's worried about trouble?" said the other Ruby twin. She playfully tugged the Commissioner's mutton-chops. "It's three weeks of Cheyenne cowboys. I'm already feeling like a worn-out mattress with a hole in it."

The Commissioner roared and pulled her onto his lap. "Ah, my sweet buttercup. Were you not illiterate I'd have you read me a dirty story."

Trixie clapped her hands and gleefully called for all to look at her seal. The animal was spinning the rubber ball on the tip of its nose. It flipped the ball up behind its back, barked, and whacked the ball with its tail. The girls cheered as the ball flew high. The dog, some six yards from the seal, leaped for the ball. It was too high-flying. It sailed above the dog's reach and looked about to sail on out the open window near Slocum. He lunged and only barely caught it.

The lunge saved his life.

A silver-handled dagger sliced over his back and stabbed into the wall.

The girls screamed. Slocum spun around, drawing his gun as he turned. The rear door of the casino was slamming shut. He might have fired a bullet through the door if a screaming girl hadn't stumbled in the way. He started to dash for the door, but a panicked girl threw her arms around him. He shrugged and dropped his gun back into its holster.

"Quiet down!" shouted the Commissioner.

It took a few minutes to calm the girls. Their screams had frightened the animals, whose yapping and barking

147

added to the noise. Through it all, Slocum calmly finished his cigar and drank the remainder of his drink. Then he pulled the dagger from the wall.

"What now, stranger?" asked the Commissioner.

"Seems only right I return Marquez his dagger."

"Could be a trap waitin' for you."

"They won't expect me to come through the front door."

The Commissioner was right behind as Slocum went back to the caboose. Slocum gave the doorknob a gentle half-turn, prepared to shoot it open were it locked. But it wasn't, and he twisted the knob hard, yanked open the door, and marched into the caboose.

Marquez was crouched over his chessboard. His hands were on the table, his bandoleer slung within easy reach over the back of his chair. His eyes looked up and met Slocum's for a moment, then returned to the chessboard.

Moy and Hip Sing were playing Mah-Jongg. The tiles were spread over the lid of Moy's trunk. Moy pretended not to notice Slocum's entrance, but a scared gurgle issued from Hip Sing's throat and his eyes darted from Slocum to the ceiling.

"Were you expecting to hear something on the roof, Hip Sing?" asked Slocum. "Is there broken glass up there to rattle out a noise? Maybe a trip-wire?"

"Welcome, my friends," said Moy. "That you choose to enter my quarters without announcing yourself makes you not unwelcome. A mere knock would have been a courtesy but— Do you play Mah-Jongg, Mr. Green?"

Marquez lifted a chess piece. "Perhaps, *senor,* you have come to play my game?"

Slocum held up the dagger. "I brought you this."

Marquez' short, greasy braids wriggled about his ears as he nodded toward the bandoleer. "As you can see, one is missing."

"We were just discussing its loss," said Moy. "We suspected a whore had stolen it."

Hip Sing tittered nervously. He sounded like a cricket, but his chirp caught in his throat when Slocum drew his gun.

"Mr. Green," said Moy. "Surely there is no need."

Slocum leveled the gun on Moy. "No moves. I see so much as a flash of your pigtail, I'll shoot it off you." He turned the gun on Marquez.

The Mexican wet his lips with his tongue. He cautiously brought up a hand and rubbed the sweat from his forehead.

"Feeling warm, Marquez?"

"When one is under the gun, *senor,* one is always hot."

"Open that side door," said Slocum. "Get a little air in here."

"If you mean to shoot me—"

Slocum fired a shot into the chessboard. The wooden pieces shattered, and a splinter the size of a toothpick stabbed Marquez's cheek.

"If I meant to shoot you, Marquez, you'd be dead. Now open the door."

Marquez carefully stood up. Slowly, he removed the splinter from his cheek and dropped it among the shattered pieces. "I carved the set myself. I was proud of it." He crossed to the door and slid it open.

Slocum threw the dagger off the train. "Go get it, Marquez."

The Mexican smiled weakly, *"Senor,* I have others."

"Go get that one," said Slocum. "If you survive the jump, you'll need the dagger to kill the rattlesnakes."

The Mexican shrugged. "It appears I have no choice." He raised his hand in a salute to Slocum, shrugged once again, and jumped.

Slocum turned his gun back to Moy and Hip Sing. Moy looked oddly amused; Hip Sing had hid his face in his hands.

"Sorry to interrupt the Mah-jongg," said Slocum. "I hear it's a fascinating game."

* * *

Slocum tossed in his sleep.

In a few hours the dragon would be leaving Cheyenne. Only a few quick stops in Nebraska were left on the schedule. The single important stop, according to Slocum, was Omaha, picking up the Indian in Omaha. Then it was on to Chicago.

Slocum began to have many sleepless nights. Han Su saw to it that he fell asleep satisfied and at peace, but Marsden had begun to invade his dreams.

Near dawn the rocking rhythm of the train would penetrate his sleep, and his body would toss and sway hotly to the rhythm. It made no difference that the train wasn't actually moving. In Slocum's dreams the dragon always moved.

A black bug the size of a hand would crawl over his face, leaving a burning track where it crawled. Cannon fire would begin—booming, roaring cannon fire. Flames exploded around him. *"Goddamn dragon's draggin' you straight to hell."* He was back at Marsden's Treachery. He and Curly Boyle and Joe Didion. They stood in the field of the dead, a field of chalk-white skulls. A fast-ridden horse bore down on them, skulls powdering under the charging hooves. Marsden whipped the horse.

"Wake up!"

Han Su was shaking him. The air was gray with the half-light of dawn.

"Someone is at the door. You must wake."

Slocum's body was damp with hot sweat. He yelled out at whoever was pounding on the door and pushed himself up from the bed. He was still groggy as he pulled on his pants.

"Who is it?" he called through the closed door.

"Commissioner."

Slocum released the latch and opened the door.

"You better come," said the Commissioner. "Moy's done killed the animals."

17

Han Su and Slocum rushed over the cindered ground toward the throng of girls who crowded near the seal's boxcar. Han Su stumbled in her haste, and cinders gouged her hands as she fell. Slocum helped her up and she hurried on, paying no attention to her scraped palms.

The girls were a subdued group. The few who weren't sobbing were holding and comforting the others. Trixie broke from the others and threw herself into Han Su's arms, crying like an injured child.

Moy and Hip Sing stood with crossed arms blocking anyone from entering the boxcar. Both wore the expression of a just-fed snake and Moy's eyes were thickly glazed. His cheeks were more heavily rouged than usual, like the cheek of an adolescent girl experimenting with makeup. He was also more animated than usual; his every movement sent a glittering slither up and down the length of his pigtail.

"It is good you have come, my cousin," Moy said to Han Su. "There has been a tragedy."

Slocum brushed past Moy and Hip Sing and looked into the car.

The few blocks of ice that hadn't melted were pushed together in the center of the car. A thin patch of gray light spilled into the cool car, and the ice had an eerie, translucent appearance. Water dripped from the ice and a black pool spread over the floor. There was the smell of blood in the air. Dark streaks stained the ice. On top of the ice were the corpses of the seal and the dog.

Slocum stepped back and put space between himself and Moy. He turned to Han Su, but his rising anger prevented him from speaking, and he gave her a look that said all she needed to know.

Trixie's face was buried against Han Su's shoulder. Wrenching sobs twisted her body. "I was coming to

151

look in on my seal. Like I do every morning. I found them just the way they are."

Han Su tenderly patted Trixie. "Did you see anyone?"

Trixie pulled back from Han Su. She still sobbed, but a look of dull shock spread across her features. "We all know who done it."

"We know nothing of the sort," said Han Su. "Unless someone saw what happened."

"My cousin," said Moy, "I arrived but moments before yourself and Mr. Green. Had I come sooner perhaps—"

"Liar!" shouted a girl.

Moy's eyes flashed and darted as he searched to find who shouted. The girls stared back at him, their faces twisted with hatred for Moy and grief at what he had done. One girl spat at the ground. Then another, one who was hidden behind the first line of girls, shouted, "We know it was you!"

"All of you!" cried Moy, "go now. You embarrass us with your grief."

"You sonofabitch," said Slocum. He took a step toward Moy, almost reaching for his gun.

Han Su read his thoughts. "Don't," she said, her voice a low, cold command.

Anger ripped through Slocum. He pointed to the boxcar. "Look! Go look at what your cousin has done."

"Mr. Green." Her voice remained cold. "No unfounded accusations."

"Take a goddamn look! Their heads are split like overripe melons. Only a cleaver could do it."

"Or an ax," said Moy. "Perhaps a western bowie knife."

"My cousin speaks correctly," Han Su said. "It is possible someone in this community wished to bring hurt upon us."

Trixie stared with horror at Han Su. "You don't believe that, Madame."

"We have no witness to this crime," said Han Su.

"Until we do, my cousin shall not be accused. Now all please leave here."

Not a single girl made a move.

Han Su clapped her hands. "Do as I say!"

"You have your orders," cried Moy. "Has *discipline* become so lax you do not obey orders!"

The girls hesitated. A number of them had suffered Moy's discipline in the past, and the rest had certainly heard stories of it. They looked at one another, as if searching among themselves for a leader to tell them what to do. Then, instead of leaving, they silently moved closer and tightened their number. One shouted to Moy, "Killer!"

"She shout!" Hip Sing jumped up and down, pointing to the girl. "She shout!"

"Bring her to me," said Moy.

Hip Sing's features lit with pleasure. He threw back his shoulders and started for the girl. Slocum stepped forward, blocking Hip Sing's way. The Chinaman tried to go around him, and Slocum reached out an open hand and slapped Hip Sing to the ground.

The girls cheered wildly. Some removed their shoes and threw them at Moy.

Moy rushed to the fallen Hip Sing, ignoring the shoes that pelted him. They exchanged a few words in Chinese and Hip Sing rose slowly and timidly to his feet. Moy moved in front of Hip Sing, as if to protect him from another slap, and stared at Slocum with a stony hatred.

"Go ahead," said Slocum. "Go for a cleaver."

Moy held the stare for a long moment. He hissed between his teeth, speaking loud enough for only Slocum to hear. "I do not move. You dare not kill me while my cousin watches. You dare not lose her favor." He threw back his head and giggled.

"Get out of here," said Slocum. "Take that trembling piece of lavender shit standing behind you and go to your goddamn caboose. Don't even come out to piss."

"But such is not possible," smiled Moy. "I have my duties to attend to."

"Do as Mr. Green says," Han Su said sharply.

Moy's face fell. A high-pitched squeak of shock came from Hip Sing. He clapped his hands against his ears and hopped from foot to foot.

Moy started to speak. "But my cousin—"

Han Su clapped her hands. "Do not argue with me."

She fixed Moy with a hard gaze. His knees appeared to weaken and he seemed to grow smaller. His thin lips twitched, his rouged cheeks flushing a deep red.

Han Su said, "Better you should feel shame, my cousin, then I should lose what respect I still have from my women. I have defended you against their unproven allegations, but I do not want you to move among them again. Mr. Green will assume your duties. You will stay in the dragon's tail unless summoned by me. Or if you prefer, you may leave the train."

"I must bear the shame you have thrust upon me." Moy's voice contained little strength. "Do not think that I have been deceived by your intentions. My shame shall not force me to leave. I stay and await my proper share."

Moy's voice withered into a senseless babble. Then he stopped and held himself tight until with a burst he flung himself to the ground, crying, "*She* did it! To do this to me, she killed them!"

Slocum and the Commissioner buried the animals.

"Why you think he did it, stranger?"

Slocum shook his head. "I'm not sure. Maybe he just smoked too much opium and went crazy."

"Ever consider maybe he didn't do it?" The Commissioner leaned against his spade waiting for Slocum's response. When none came, the Commissioner said, "Why don't you jus' kill him?"

"I gave my word."

The Commissioner chortled. "Ain't you ever broke it?"

"Only when I've had to."

"Supposin' Moy stays put 'til Chicago? Will you have to then?"

Slocum used the blade of his spade to tamp the mound of the grave. "I hope not."

"Ain't you forgettin' somethin'? Moy's still got a trunk of opium to buy an army with."

"I haven't forgotten."

18

The Indian, whose name was Red Bear, wore a heavy necklace of quartz stones and bear claws. He traveled with a ten-year-old boy, whose name was never given. He held the boy's hand as the two of them made their way through the crowded Omaha depot and approached Slocum and the Commissioner. He walked as if unaware of all the curious bystanders who stared and pointed at him.

"Good God," muttered the Commissioner.

The necklace was the only thing about the Indian that looked *Indian*. He was tall, but stooped shoulders and a shuffling walk made him appear average in height. He wore the clothing of a white man, clothing so tattered it might have been stolen from a scarecrow. His hands shook, his hair was matted and filthy, his face looked like someone had taken it apart and put it back together without quite making the pieces fit. Worst of all were his eyes—his colorless, opaque, blind eyes.

"I was told you want to know of Peshtigo," the Indian said. "I will help all I can. But first, my grandchild has not eaten for two days."

There was a thin rattle in the timbre of the Indian's voice. The rattle sounded both definite and hesitant. Slocum had heard the same tone in the voices of certain men who had lost everything in the war, men too proud to forget what they had possessed, yet still ashamed by the loss.

155

"Hell," the Commissioner said, "we'll feed the both of you."

The Indian straightened his stooped shoulders and attempted to reach his full height. The weight of his necklace appeared to hold him down. The withered lines of his broken face stretched tight as he pushed out his jaw, and there was no hint of a question in his voice when he said, "Do you have whiskey!"

Slocum told the Commissioner, "Go tell Mr. Peasly to move out. Then bring the madame to the dining car."

The Commissioner gruffly whispered in Slocum's ear, "Hell, give 'em food. But why waste time talkin' to a blind drunk?"

"Do what you're told!" snapped Slocum. "I don't want these damn gawkers listening in on me."

"Sure, yell at me," muttered the Commissioner. "But you ever know an alkie who knew dif'rent 'tween truth an' his last drink?"

Slocum led the boy and the Indian into the train and to the dining car. He got them seated at a table and ordered food.

The Indian's hands shook against the table. His voice rattled as he stoutly thrust out his jaw and said, "I asked for whiskey."

"You shall have it, Red Bear," said Slocum with a grim shake of his head. One thing was purely sure, he wasn't going to get a map out of a blind man.

He got a bottle, poured a large whiskey, and placed one of the Indian's shaking hands around the glass. After two deep swallows the Indian's hands lost their shake. Slocum refilled the glass.

The food arrived at the same time Han Su and the Commissioner joined the table. Though he'd expressed no desire for food, Red Bear's broken features twisted with hunger as he smelled the plate sitting before him. He seemed to be fighting a battle with himself, as if he genuinely didn't want to eat, but hunger finally won. He leaned low and scooped up the food with his fingers, cleaning the plate within two minutes. He declined the Commissioner's cheerful offer of a second serving. "We would be grateful for any food to take with us," he said.

"You may take all you wish," said Han Su.

Red Bear reacted sharply to the sound of Han Su's voice. "Is woman chief here?"

"I am chief," said Slocum. He shot Han Su a glance, warning her to say no more. "It pleases me to have my woman at my council table."

"I understand," nodded Red Bear. "I always took pleasure in women, too."

The train lurched and started to move.

Red Bear gripped the edge of the table. The lids of his sightless eyes blinked rapidly, and he reached for his grandchild. "You take me to Peshtigo!" he said, his voice full of fear.

"No," said Slocum. He leaned across the table and placed a firm hand on the Indian's shoulder. "We do not take you there. Our train must keep moving. After we finish our talk, we will stop at the nearest station and let you and your grandchild off. We will give you much food."

"Why you scared o' Peshtigo?" asked the Commissioner. "Come from there, don't you?"

The Indian's hands were shaking again. He reached for his drink, but Slocum snatched the glass away. The Indian's hands fumbled with desperation over the table.

"Answer the man, Red Bear," said Slocum.

"Fear does not keep me from my homeland."

"Is it because you're a drunk?" asked Slocum. "And your people threw you out because they don't like drunks?"

"No."

"And now to get a drink, you'd tell a person just about anything, wouldn't you?"

"No!" The Indian thrust his fingers against his sightless eyes. "What I feel is worse than fear. Worse than hatred. It is why I am this way."

"What is it?" asked the Commissioner.

An agonized moan gushed from the Indian's throat. "I was a chief."

"Marsden!" The boy leaped up and tore his grandfather's drink from Slocum's hand. He gave the drink to his grandfather, put his arms around his grandfather's head and rocked him while the old man choked down his whiskey. "Marsden made him this way!"

Han Su bit her lips to keep from calling out.

"I'll be a sonofabitch," muttered the Commissioner.

Slocum nodded. He filled glasses for himself and the Commissioner. He reached over and filled the Indian's glass. "Red Bear, there's something you ought to know. We're going to Wisconsin to kill Marsden."

Red Bear told his story.

His people had lived in Wisconsin since before the birth of the legends. The very name given to the state was their word meaning gathering of the waters. They were a peaceful people. There was no reason for them not to be, as the heavens had given them an abundance of blessings. Their forests were vast and bountiful with game, their rivers and lakes rich with fish, their streams plentiful with rice. In all the years they had shared their land with the white man, only twice did Red Bear's tribe raise arms against them. The first was during the white man's War of 1812, when Red Bear's grandfather was chief, and the tribe fought on the side of the British. The second was when Red Bear led a raid against Marsden.

Before Marsden came, Peshtigo was only a tiny settlement that had grown around a trading post. A few whites had planted farms in the isolated forest clearings surrounding the settlement. Red Bear's tribe lived in a village some miles north.

The tribe got along fine with the whites. They had been getting along with whites ever since Red Bear's ancestors had greeted the first French explorers two hundred years before. Members of the tribe regularly went into Peshtigo and traded skins and pelts for certain goods and wares they had come to depend on. They never felt cheated.

The tribe had watched the farmers cut a few trees to build their homes and clear their fields, but the forest was big and would not miss a scattering of trees. No one could possibly cut the entire forest—no one would want to—and if the whites preferred to sweat and toil to dig their food from the ground, well that was the white way.

One evening Red Bear had stood on the Green Bay shore. He looked across the waters to the peninsula at the other side and remembered the legend of the peninsula.

The legend told of a long ago battle between two tribes. The battle had taken place in the strait separating the tip of the peninsula from an island. On a dark night, in the midst of a rainless summer, each tribe had set out in its canoes to attack the other. Their canoes met, the battle began, and in the heat of it, the heavens sent down an immense storm and all the warriors perished. Since that night, legend said, the strait had become the door through which death walked.

With the memory of the legend, Red Bear had fallen to the ground, shivering violently. The heavens had sent him a warning, but he did not recognize it, and the next morning Marsden arrived in Peshtigo and sought him out.

"I'm a friend of the redman, Chief. I have come to offer your people much wealth. The city of Chicago needs lumber. I mean to supply that lumber. Your people start to work in the morning building my mill. I expect my mill ready to cut the logs I'll be floating come spring. I'll be paying honest wages for honest work. I'll be building schools to educate your children, a hospital for your sick, and there will be a church for those of you who want to follow the true God."

Marsden's arrogance was so completely alien to Red Bear that Red Bear had laughed and asked, "What if my people do not want to work for you, or accept what you offer?"

"If you want to keep living in your heathen primordial mud, that's up to you. I don't hold with ungodly slavery. I'll bring in outsiders. The state of Wisconsin is behind me, the federal government is behind me, God is behind me. If I weren't a friend of the redman I wouldn't be giving you this chance to crawl into civilization."

"You want us to help you cut the forest, our home?"

"Not the whole damn thing! I only mean to harvest some of this crop planted by God. He didn't plant it just so your people can romp around like Adam before the Fall. There's a nation to be built. His nation! Timber is needed."

Red Bear called a council meeting. It lasted through the night. Going to war with Marsden was out of the question. The tribe had been at peace too long and didn't know how to fight. Since Marsden planned to cut the trees anyway, why shouldn't they take the offered wages instead of letting outsiders get the money. Enough of the tribe had experienced white man's money to know its value. And how many trees could Marsden cut? The forest was big. It would require all the seasons of all the men of the tribe to cut even those trees that grew around Peshtigo, let alone the whole surrounding forest. They decided to take the work.

Their decision made them like the man who pisses on the hill above his water. He does not notice as the water gradually loses its sweetness. Then one day it kills him.

Marsden soon owned all of Peshtigo. Anything the Indians needed—equipment to do his work, or goods they had always traded for in the past—had to be bought from his store. He gave them credit and took what he said they owed from their wages. If they questioned him about bills, he showed them pages of numbers which they did not understand.

No sooner was the mill finished than Marsden brought in Scandinavian and German loggers and sawyers. The outsiders received more pay than the Indians. Red Bear protested.

"Chief, they're Christians with families to support. Your people don't need as much money as them. It's a sad thing you reds can't get along with civilized men. I'm going to have to separate the camps. This season I want your braves to open up new sites to the north."

There in the train's dining car, his sightless eyes staring into nothingness, his gnarled old hands nursing his whiskey glass, Red Bear told of all the false promises, all the indignities the Indians had suffered under Marsden. Marsden had them in his economic thumbscrew, and every season he tightened the pressure.

"The only cheap thing was whiskey," Red Bear said. "A drunken Indian is easily controlled."

Marsden had the threat of government power behind him, and whenever Red Bear protested the opening of a new logging site, Marsden threatened intervention by the government.

"But he had a simpler means of keeping things his way," Red Bear said. "His outsiders were as unhappy with their conditions as were we Indians. He told them our cheap labor was responsible for their low pay. Thus, every white came to see us as an enemy, and they used every opportunity to humiliate us and sometimes to beat us."

One day Marsden called Red Bear to his home. He had built the largest house in Peshtigo. Red Bear told how Marsden had invited him into his office. The most impressive things about the office, Red Bear said, were the huge safe where he kept his money and a large wall map of the forest.

"Red Bear, sit down," Marsden had said. "Here, have some good whiskey for a change. I notice some of your people have taken too much to the white man's drink."

"It is about all they can afford."

"Wouldn't be true if they learned to use their money properly. All the problems between us would be settled

161

if you people would join the nineteenth century. Education is what you need. You've got a couple of grandchildren. The girl, how old is she now?"

"Fourteen summers. Her younger brother is—"

"Send them to me. Isn't right for a chief's descendants to be running around barefoot, half-educated. I'll have a private tutor for them here. When they're ready, I'll send them to a university and when they come back, Chief, they'll have the proper knowledge to lead your people right."

"My grandchildren stay with their parents."

"You have it your way, Chief. Now let's get down to business. You've about twenty or so young bucks who are starting to behave like Apaches. One of them, your own son. As you know, he had to be horsewhipped last week. I have to get some of the goddamn heathen savagery out of him. This is Wisconsin, not the Wild West. I'm not going to allow any Indian war here."

Marsden had stood up then, near the map. It was stuck with pins with little flags marking the various logging sites. There were over forty pins. Marsden pointed to a spot on the map.

"You take your wild bucks and open up this new site. Keep them up there through the winter and let them cool off. Naturally, to keep my white workers satisfied you aren't getting something belonging to them, I'll have one of my Scandinavians with you as overseer."

Red Bear protested, "That place is seventy miles away."

"My reports tell me the white pine there is so tall it scratches God's backside. I want that pine."

"How much further you plan to go!"

"Far as God means me to!"

"Already your pins surround our village."

"I'll jab a pin right into your village and start cutting in the morning if you don't do what I say. You have fought me every inch of the way, Red Bear. I'm a man, and as God is my witness, I can tolerate your belligerence to me but I cannot tolerate your fighting

162

progress. Look at my map and tell me how much of your precious forest I have cut. It amounts to less than a pimple on your red ass! Now look out my window. Won't be long before Peshtigo is a metropolis. I'm building my own railroad next year. Plenty of opportunity for you Indians to learn new work skills if you so care. Learn professions! Join the world! Else you better pick up your village and move deeper into the forest."

"I will take my young men and open your new site. I don't want them to suffer any more whippings. In the spring, my people will leave here. You have changed in a few years what we have known for hundreds."

"Go. It will be a damn sight easier for me without you. But if you cared about the future of your people you would leave your grandchildren with me. You can hide in the wilderness and be worm feed before civilization catches you. They can't!"

There was a series of accidents at the new logging site. Twice Red Bear almost lost his life. Then came an accident that killed his son.

"We knew it was not a true accident," Red Bear said. "We killed the Scandinavian overseer and returned to our village."

Marsden had begun cutting the trees near their village. When Red Bear went to tell his daughter-in-law about the death of her husband, he learned Marsden had taken his grandchildren. He rode into town to get them.

"I tied my horse to the hitching post in front of his house," Red Bear said. "The post was shaped and painted to resemble a black servant boy. I knocked on the door. It was answered by my grandson, the boy who sits here with me now. He was dressed to look like the hitching post."

Red Bear had stormed into Marsden's office.

"What the hell you doing back, Chief?"

"I have come for my grandchildren."

"Take them. The boy's a fine enough worker, once he felt the strap a few times. As for the girl, she's an

163

embarrassment to me. I did my best for her. She repaid me by getting herself a belly full of child. Damned if I'll allow a half-breed heathen to run around my house!"

Red Bear took the children back to his village. He and the twenty men who had been at the new camp put on warpaint.

"We would not allow others to join us," he said. "We knew our raid would cause the government to send in troops, and we did not want all the tribe to suffer for our deed. We were prepared to die. We hoped to kill Marsden and burn his mill before meeting death."

The raid was a total failure. They managed to set a few fires at the outskirts of town, but the fires were extinguished before doing any great damage. They didn't kill a single white, their own number was quickly cut down, and they were forced to surrender.

"We rode in with the wild whoops legends told us our ancestors used," Red Bear said. "They let us get close, then they fired their shotguns. Only six of us survived. They tied and marched us to Marsden's house. The white men thought our raid very funny. To them, it was like a big Saturday night. Marsden was waiting for us on his front lawn."

"Red Bear, you're responsible for the most unholy, perfidious act of treachery I've ever known. Were you reds civilized, you would be entitled to a trial. Since you're savages, I must deal with you savagely. Your men will be hanged in the morning. As for yourself, Red Bear, your punishment shall fit with the blind actions of your crime. No Indian shall ever look on you without seeing the example of your blind ways. I'm going to have your eyelids sewn open. I personally am going to hold before you the flaming brand of truth until you are as sightless as your atheistic beliefs."

Han Su had begun trembling with rage as Red Bear reached the end of his story. The Commissioner was looking sick and, for a change, had nothing to say. The

164

boy picked up the whiskey and poured his grandfather another drink.

Slocum said, "How long ago did this happen, Red Bear?"

"By your calendar, I was blinded a year and a half ago."

"And you've not been back to Peshtigo since?"

Red Bear nodded. "I am kept informed. Much has changed. Bring to me a map, paper and a pen. I will describe the town and my grandson will draw what I describe. On the map he will make lines of trails known only to Indians. After you kill Marsden you must set a false trail west. The law will follow that trail while you go north. You will meet Indians and show them this necklace, which I will leave with you. They will help you through Michigan and on to Canada."

The Commissioner went to fetch a map and drawing equipment.

Slocum asked, "Why does Marsden keep his money in a safe in his house? Isn't there a bank in Peshtigo?"

Red Bear threw back his drink and laughed bitterly. "There is the Marsden Trust and Loan. Maybe he cannot afford to pay what he charges others to keep their money. Rob the bank. Rob his shipping office. Rob his mill. His safe in his home will have more money than all those others combined."

"I didn't say we were going to rob anybody," said Slocum.

Red Bear slapped the table. "If you are going to kill him you would be stupid not to take what is there. Others in the town will loot what you do not take. Give me more whiskey."

Slocum filled the Indian's glass again. "What kind of security does Marsden have?'"

"A few police. They are not paid well, but they are the kind of men who enjoy the power he allows them more than they care for money. Troops will come up from Green Bay in an emergency, but Green Bay is many hours distant, and the telegraph wire is easily cut."

"How many people in the town?"

"Over two thousand live there always. We are in your calendar month of September and that means an additional two thousand, maybe more—loggers who are waiting for the season to begin. And all the railroad workers."

"The railroad in operation?"

"Only part finished," said Red Bear with a shake of his head. "The men have refused to work since July."

The Commissioner returned. "Here's what you folks need to plan up what I'd rather be surprised by. See you all in the mornin'!"

Slocum took the map from the Commissioner. He glanced at the man, somewhat taken aback by his lack of interest.

The Commissioner winked. "I've an assignation with a Ruby twin. Promised her the best meal in Chicago. She's promised not to point her finger and laugh." He went out and into the next car.

Slocum opened the map and placed it in front of the boy. He said to Red Bear, "So there's two thousand men either idle or on strike."

Red Bear nodded. "They spend their time drinking and fighting. Indians are afraid to come into town. No white woman who is not a whore walks the streets after sundown. Marsden's false promises are the source of their unhappiness. He depends on them fighting each other instead of attacking him."

"How many whorehouses?"

"Marsden does not allow them, but there are women who sell themselves. He allows enough to stay to keep the men on edge, but not enough to satisfy. It is another way to keep them fighting each other."

"Sounds like maybe the free enterprise system in Peshtigo needs a helping hand," said Slocum with a grin.

"There is also a drought. No rain since July. The

166

pines are yellowed, their needles stiff as splinters. The air is ever dry as noon dust. The man who wishes to bathe can fill a tub more cheaply with whiskey than with fresh water. There is the river, but Marsden punishes those caught naked in the river with a fine and a public whipping. For once our medicine men and the white preachers are in agreement. Both say the heavens have sent the drought to punish Peshtigo for its wickedness."

"I'm no avenging angel," laughed Slocum. "But I'll be punishing Marsden right soon. Now let's start drawing pictures, Red Bear."

The Indian spoke for three hours. Slocum listened and watched the boy draw and silently made plans. When the Indian had finished, Slocum had only a few final questions.

"It sounds damn good," he said with satisfaction. "We will pay you well for this information, Red Bear."

"When I hear you have been successful, it will be payment enough."

"Whatever you say, Red Bear," said Slocum, gesturing to Han Su that she give money to the boy. "It is late now. My woman will make you and your grandson comfortable for the rest of this night. I will see you before you leave."

"You must not forget this." Red Bear took off his necklace and handed it to Slocum.

Slocum left the dining car. By this time tomorrow they would be in Chicago, and there was no need to make rounds. But the Indian's information had given him such a sense of exhilaration that he wanted to walk.

Everyone on the train was alseep; there was a fine, quiet peace to the night. As he passed between cars he noticed the sweet dew-fresh odor of the Iowa countryside. When the train twisted for a curve, he caught a glimpse of the dragon's tail. There were no lights visible, but its black silhouette cut into the dark sky. He had a plan for the tail, too. He chuckled softly to himself and put the Indian's necklace around his neck. Its solid

167

weight felt good. It was a good night for plans. For a moment he had an urge to cup his hands to his mouth and shout out a wild Indian whoop.

He continued through the train. Stepping easily along the steel walkways separating the cars, he realized that he had become as accustomed to the vibrating rhythm of the train as he was to sitting a horse.

He met nobody until he entered the first casino and found a Ruby twin playing solitaire.

"Howdy, Mr. Green. Looks like we made it, huh?"

"More than you know, honey. What are your plans after Chicago?"

She shrugged. "See a few shows, head back west." She reached up and touched the necklace around his neck. "Pretty. I like a man who ain't afraid to wear pretty things."

"I'm going to be offering you girls a proposition. If all goes well, come another month, you'll be a rich lady."

She ran her hand over his chest. "A proposition. Uh-huh." She put her hand to her hair and fluffed it, then picked up her cards and began to shuffle them lazily. "Know what would make me feel right rich? To spread my legs for a real man and think about nothin' 'cept the pleasure I'm giving and gettin'. I'm tired of the life. Here it is soul time in the a.m. and I'm alone with a deck of cards. Trip's been okay, but I don't want to ride any more dragons."

He touched her cheek lightly. "Sounds like you want to settle down and get respectable."

"I don't give a shit about respect. Just want a life without a Moy."

"Money buys that."

"Won't buy a real man, Mr. Green. Won't buy you. Wish I'd seen you before the madame did." She twisted her lips into a parody of her professional smile and winked. "Don't reckon you'd be interested in a slice from a cut loaf?"

168

"Not tonight," he laughed. "Where's the Commissioner? He was feeling randy earlier."

"He wandered through a while ago." Wearily, she began to deal herself a new hand of solitaire. "Promised me a thousand pornographic delights if I'd join him in the saloon for a nightcap."

Slocum went into the saloon, but it was empty. On the bar a half-full bottle and an empty glass gave mute testimony that the Commissioner had been there. The rear door was partially open. A shapeless mass on the floor was wedged between the door and the frame, something that looked like it might be a cushion from one of the seats. Slocum started through the car. He had taken only a few steps before he realized the mass holding open the door was one of the Commissioner's legs.

He hurried to where the man lay, pulling the door full open and almost stumbling over the thin wire which had tripped the Commissioner.

The man lay face down on the walkway of the saloon car. The safety straps had been removed. It must have been something of a miracle that when he stumbled he hadn't fallen off the train. Slocum turned him over. There was only a small bruise on his forehead. His eyes were closed, his mouth slightly open. Slocum breathed with relief, telling himself the Commissioner was merely unconscious. Then he put his fingers to the man's head. It was like touching mud.

The Commissioner's skull had been crushed between the walkways. A later lurch of the train had knocked his murdered corpse into the position where Slocum had found him.

19

They turned off onto a siding and buried the Commissioner in the rolling green of Iowa farmland. Mr. Peasly read the words. The service was short and unsentimental, and near the end of it Han Su began to weep.

Moy and Hip Sing attended the funeral. They stood a fair distance from the others. Hip Sing continually, nervously, glanced at Slocum. Moy kept a steel hard expression that was both bored and contemptuous.

When the coffin had been lowered in all the girls threw a handful of dirt into the grave. Han Su had declared it a day of mourning. The train would not move for twenty-four hours, and while the girls left the grave site she lingered behind with Slocum and Peasley, who were to finish the burying.

Moy approached her. "My cousin, while the Commissioner's death was an unfortunate accident, I feel it serves no purpose for our dragon to sit idle."

"Leave me alone, Moy," said Han Su.

"Has the fact that you have learned to weep like a woman destroyed your sense of business?"

Slocum reached into his pocket and took out a coil of wire. He tossed it at Moy's feet. "The only accident, Moy, was the Commissioner stumbling over that wire instead of me."

Moy looked down at the wire. "Why, Mr. Green, do you insist on laying the blame for misfortune at my feet?"

"I don't think you stretched the wire, Moy. I think you told Hip Sing to do it."

Hip Sing jerked back and half hid himself behind Moy.

"It resembles the wire of a whore's corset," said Moy. He looked at Han Su. "Have you questioned the whores?"

Han Su lunged forward and scraped her nails down Moy's cheek. Slocum drew his gun as Moy thrust her away.

Moy put his hand to his ripped cheek and looked with horror at the blood on his fingers. Hip Sing rushed around in front of Moy and began dabbing Moy's scratches with a handkerchief.

"Get back to your caboose," ordered Slocum.

"Pull your trigger, Mr. Green," spat Moy. "Is not the grave already dug? Have you not already tried and convicted me?"

"I wouldn't dishonor the Commissioner by throwing your bodies on top of his," Slocum said. "I'd leave you for the birds."

"Enough!" cried Han Su. She turned and ran stumbling through the grassy field, her shoulders heaving with sobs.

"Now, Mr. Green," said Moy, "we show you our backs. If you wish to shoot us—"

Slocum kept his gun on Moy and Hip Sing until they were well on their way back to the caboose. Then he and Mr. Peasly finished filling the Commissioner's grave.

"Why didn't you kill them?" asked Mr. Peasly.

"Mr. Peasly, I think it's time we discussed the future of the rails of America."

"What do you mean?"

"I mean," said Slocum, "doing something about that tail."

When Slocum had finished at the grave, he followed in the direction Han Su had gone. He went nearly a mile before he found her hidden in a patch of tall grass. He got down on the ground beside her and took her in his arms.

"I loved that old man," she wept.

He put his lips to her eyes and kissed her tears. He held her close until her body ceased trembling with grief.

"I love you, John Slocum," she said. She curled up against his chest.

He picked a blade of grass and traced it along the lines of her face. "Now I'll tell you the plans for Peshtigo," he said. "And at a certain time tomorrow, I want Moy to join us and I'll tell him his part."

"I no longer care if you kill him."

171

"You don't this minute. But your family sense of honor is there and a week from now, or a year, you would care."

"Make love to me, John Slocum."

They had Moy sit down with them in the dining room, at the same table where the Indian had sat. Moy was alone, because Slocum had said he didn't want Hip Sing in on the conversation.

Slocum wasted no time. "You're coming to Peshtigo with us, Moy."

Moy shook his head. "I wish only to take the money due me and leave you."

"You've no choice," said Slocum. "You want a share, you'll get it after Peshtigo."

"I have no fight with Marsden. I do not wish to go there."

"You're not listening," continued Slocum. "Your share of the sale of the dragon is going to finance Peshtigo. We're converting your money into wagons and tents. You're also going to have to cut your pigtail. Marsden would likely recognize that slimy braid and we can't risk it."

Moy's thin lips fell open with disbelief. "You think to cut my——?" He shook his head rapidly and babbled protests in both English and Chinese. When he tried to stand and leave he found Slocum blocking his way.

"Look out the window," said Slocum. "We're about to cross the Mississippi River. Means we're officially east."

Moy looked at Han Su. "He talks to me of rivers, while in the same breath suggests to cut my pigtail. My face still burns with the shame of your nails tearing my flesh. I shall suffer no more."

"We cannot allow you not to come with us, Moy," Han Su said. "Once you served Marsden with loyalty. I fear you would try to warn him of our coming. If you do exactly as you are told, you will be treated fairly and receive a full share, just as all the girls who come

172

with us are receiving a full share. Your alternative is to be killed."

Moy sank back in his chair, his features drained and pale as milk. The train started to cross over the bridge of the Mississippi. Moy's voice struggled from somewhere deep in his chest. "You stoop to treating me as an equal with a whore?"

The scaffolding of the bridge shook with the weight of the train. Below them the river was brown with mud and speckled with patches of floating green algae. The train moved with a hollow, rumbling rhythm. It appeared to pick up speed as the engine left the bridge and began to climb the steep, curving bluff on the far side of the river.

Han Su steadied her hands on the table and said with alarm, "Is Mr. Peasley not going too fast?"

"He needs a good head of steam to climb the bluffs," explained Slocum.

Because of the angle of the curve, they were able to see from their window the rear half of the train come off the bridge. The green tail careened around the curve, the high arch looking like it was whipping loose from the roof of the caboose. Actually, the caboose itself was snapping loose from the train. It shuddered there alone on the track for a moment, then, so slowly that it looked like a paper kite being tossed by a soft breeze, the dragon's tail tumbled over and rolled down the banks of the bluff into the Mississippi.

Moy's eyes widened with shock. He pushed his way past Slocum and ran to the exit. Mr. Peasley was braking the train, but Moy leaped out before it came to a full stop and tore his way back to where the caboose was sinking—slowly, steadily sinking into the river.

Han Su turned away from the window. She stared down at her hands folded in her lap. "Was it necessary, John Slocum?"

He didn't bother answering her. He left the dining car and went to a supply car and got himself a coil of rope. He deftly knotted the rope into a lasso noose as he casually sauntered down to join the others at the river bank.

Only the very top of the tail could be seen above the water. White foam swirled around it. A trace of green algae clung to it like a loosened scale.

Moy was frantically running up and down the bank, calling for somebody, anybody, to do something. "You!" he shouted as Slocum approached. "You use your rope. You save Hip Sing!"

Slocum twirled the lasso in lazy loops over his head. "I'm afraid Hip Sing is food for the fish, Moy. So is whatever else you had in that tail."

Slocum tossed out the rope with a light flick of his wrist. The lasso looped neatly down over Moy's shoulders and Slocum pulled it tight. Moy started to fall. Slocum threw slack into the rope, then gave it a couple of twists and by the time Moy hit the ground his arms were immobilized by rope.

Slocum straddled the Chinaman's thin chest, reached up one of Moy's sleeves and pulled out a cleaver. He raised the cleaver high, and Moy screeched and writhed like a trapped bug. Then Slocum brought down the cleaver and cut off Moy's pigtail.

Slocum threw the pigtail into the river.

Moy lay silent and shivering. His eyes, which had so often been waxy and evil, were now nothing but glazed little capsules of crippled fear.

20

They entered Peshtigo on a Saturday morning in October. A wall of pine, oak and tamarack surrounded the town, but there was no fresh smell of a forest and the air was dry with a dust as fine as ash.

They arrived in eight brightly painted circus wagons, every wagon pulled by four horses—former saddle mounts groomed and harnessed to resemble team

174

horses. The Barnum people had been happy to provide the horses and wagons, plus other needed equipment, as part payment for the dragon. They had brought twenty girls with them, ten of whom Slocum had given lessons on how to blow open a safe. Slocum feared more than twenty girls would slow up their Sunday night escape.

Slocum drove the first wagon. Han Su sat beside him. She gripped his thigh with excitement and waved gaily to the crowds who had appeared within minutes of their arrival. Moy was huddled inside the wagon, his teeth chattering with the chill of opium withdrawal. An iron collar around his neck was attached to a chain anchored to the wagon floor.

"Eye, mistah!" shouted a man with a rolling Scandinavian accent. "Vot you brought us in da vay-gons?"

"You know Schmidt's Clearing just outside of town?" answered Slocum.

"Ya. Ve cut dat dere years ago."

"Ride out there come sunset, friend."

The town looked one day old and a century dying. The first thing they passed was a field of stubbled grass filled with the tents and shacks and lean-tos of the striking railroad workers. Black fumes lifted from the pitchfires around which the men were cooking their breakfasts, and the fumes hung in a rancid mist above the field. Hundreds of strikers rushed through it to greet the wagons, shouting and banging their tin plates with spoons. The wagons rolled on past the unfinished railroad depot and from there on into town the road was lined with wooden sidewalks.

The town was divided in half by the Peshtigo River. This side of the river was mainly residential, those who lived here primarily laborers. The wagons passed numerous boardinghouses, all hung with "No Vacancy" signs. They passed wooden-shingled houses, the shingles flaking dusty gray chips, and there were unpainted, rough plank houses that looked the color of a thirsty yellow dog. Other buildings were under construction. The din of construction was halted as the

175

carpenters put down their tools to greet and follow the wagons.

They had to wait at the river for ferries to take them across. White waiting, Slocum threw out cards he'd had printed in Chicago. The cards read, *"Schmidt's Clearing, Spirituous Likker & Wimmen of Spirit."*

"Whiskey we got!" shouted a man wearing the laced high boots of a lumberjack. "Did you bring water?"

"Barrels of it," said Slocum. "One dollar for the first tub, two-bits for used water."

The crowd cheered.

"But if you boys want your back scrubbed by a pretty woman, that's an extra charge." Slocum stood up and gestured to the wagons behind. "Any man here want to work? I've tents to pitch and a camp to set up. Pays two dollars an hour!"

With shouts of, "We'll be waitin' for you," men charged into the river. Some had animals to carry them but most swam.

It was an hour getting all eight wagons across the river. The crowds awaiting them were as large and noisy as those on the other side.

As the wagons moved up Main Street, two fire-and-brimstone preachers broke from the crowded sidewalks. One shouted "Sin! Sin! Sin!" while the other pounded a bass drum on the side of which was painted "Redemption is Rain." A burly logger leaped out to scare away the preachers.

The saloons were all busy despite the morning hour, but a number of the stores, though open for business, had broken and boarded-over windows. A sign on the Marsden Company store read, "Strikers Not Welcome." Slocum noticed with satisfaction that most of the animals tied to the hitching posts were slow mules or workhorses.

The largest building was the mill. It loomed up at the outer edge of the town, a crude and ugly structure. The only other buildings of any size were the Forest House hotel, which stood in the center of Main Street, and

Marsden's house. It was a white-frame castle on a high hill overlooking the town.

Slocum pointed out the house to Han Su. "You can bet he's watching us from one of his windows."

She gripped his arm and stared up at the house. "How soon before he approaches us?"

No sooner had she spoken than a line of ten men, all wearing ill-fitting blue uniforms, derby hats with stars pinned to them and handlebar mustaches, stepped out to block the road. They carried sawed-off shotguns, and heavy clubs swung from their belts.

"Consider yourself approached," Slocum chuckled. He halted the wagon.

One of the uniformed men slowly strutted forward. The word "chief" was imprinted on a star pinned to his derby.

"Howdy," said Slocum with a wide and friendly grin. "Reckon you're the police."

The chief nodded.

"Well," said Slocum, "that's a right smart looking force."

"We do our job," said the chief, moving his shotgun from one shoulder to the other. He craned his neck for a glance down the line of wagons. "Just who are you people? What are you doing in Peshtigo?"

"Name's Green. This lady beside me is my wife."

The policeman blinked and looked closely at Han Su. "You married to *her?*"

"We are circus people," said Han Su. "Move your men and let us be on our way."

"On your way to where?" snarled the chief. "There's no place to go from here." He hunched his shoulders and started walking down the line of wagons.

Han Su put her hands to her mouth and giggled softly to Slocum, "If in New York we decide to marry, do not give me the name of Green."

"After tomorrow," Slocum said out of the side of his mouth, "it might be fitting if we named ourselves after this town."

177

She whispered, "You still think tomorrow is not too soon?"

"A rat needs time to smell the cheese," Slocum said. "If I thought we could lure him out sooner, I'd move tonight."

The chief returned, cradling his shotgun in his arm. He tilted back his derby and brushed back the ends of his mustache. "Your wagons are full of women. Don't look like circus people at all. Look like wantons."

"How dare you!" snapped Han Su with haughty indignation. She stood up and spat at the chief's feet.

The chief jumped as if he'd been shot at, and the men in line all shifted their shotguns into firing position. Slocum wasn't worried. He was confident the police were under orders not to fire.

"Green," frowned the chief, "you tell your wife my business is with you and not her."

"Move your men," Slocum said coolly. "We're on our way to Schmidt's Clearing. I don't want to ride over them."

Sweat popped out on the chief's forehead. His eyes darted with confusion toward the white house on the hill. "You can't put up your so called circus in the clearing."

"It stands outside of your town limits."

"Only a hundred yards."

"That puts it out of your jurisdiction."

"But—"

"Drive on, my husband," Han Su said regally.

Slocum slapped the reins. As the wagon started forward, the chief glumly ordered his men to let them pass.

The camp went up so quickly that Slocum had to create jobs for all the men who wanted work. He set one group to digging slit latrines and another to cutting trees and building a split-rail corral. A third group he put to work as cooks. Soon he noticed a large percentage of the men looked to a heavyset, robust man named Fritz for a nod of approval before setting to a

178

new task. When Slocum learned Fritz was a leader of the rail strike, he made him his foreman.

The first thing Fritz asked Slocum was, "Is the rumor true?"

"What rumor?"

"That you and your Mrs. intend to start your own logging operation?"

"Well, hell, Fritz, I—" Slocum broke off and stuttered for words.

Han Su stepped forward. "My husband, perhaps we should be careful what we say."

"Quite right, dear." Slocum looked Fritz straight in the eye. "We've no definite plans."

Shortly after their arrival, Slocum took food and water to Moy. He unlocked the door of the wagon and climbed in, giving his eyes a second to adjust to the dim interior before approaching the chained Moy.

"Use your fingers," he said, placing the plate on the floor in front of the Chinaman. "I'm not risking you trying to gouge my eyes out with a chopstick."

Moy shivered. "I am sick. I cannot eat."

"I'm not leaving you the tin plate and cup to bend into weapons."

"Better you should have killed me."

"I wanted to. I just decided there was something I wanted more."

Moy lifted the cup of water, spilling half of it before it reached his mouth. "A thousand needles pierce me. Surely there is a pharmacy near. Bring what I need. I promise on my ancestors to protect you from her."

"In Canada you'll get a horse and more money than you deserve," Slocum said. "That's all."

When Slocum reached for the plate and cup, Moy lunged, but his weakened condition made the lunge pathetic. Slocum effortlessly avoided the Chinaman's reach. The chain cracked at its bolt, and Moy fell back, clawing at his collar.

* * *

For the rest of the afternoon, Slocum and Han Su watched their "circus" being built around them. They also watched the road leading back to town, but it remained empty.

"Marsden won't come himself," said Slocum. "He'll send someone else."

"If he does not?"

"If it gets to be nine o'clock, we'll meet him halfway by riding into town and ordering dinner at the Forest House hotel."

"And if still he does not contact us?"

"You know he will."

"I know we have depended upon his greed. Until now I have not worried."

The late afternoon sun was an arid, yellow ball when Fritz reported to them that all the work was done.

"The boys would like their pay now," said Fritz. "Been a good while since most of them had other than Marsden script. They'd like to get back to town and buy vittles for the family pot."

"Hell, Fritz," smiled Slocum, "we've plenty of food. Tell them to bring their families out here for dinner."

"By all means," added Han Su. "We owe you men much."

"Two dollars an hour is what you owe them, ma'am," Fritz said. "No offense meant, but lot of these boys don't think this is quite the place they want their families. I suspect, though, they'll most all be coming back later."

Slocum nodded with understanding. "You a family man, Fritz?"

Fritz shook his head with a grim laugh. "If I had a family I wouldn't dare lead a strike against Marsden."

"Then maybe yourself, maybe a few others you might know, would care to work through the night as private guards. We want everybody to have a good time but—"

Fritz held up his hands. "Don't worry, Mr. Green. You'll have boys out here blowin' off a hot summer's worth of steam. Your fresh barrels of water will be sold by midnight. But nobody will do you wrong. You maybe don't realize it, but you and your Mrs. have done a heck of a lot for Peshtigo today. I'd be proud to work for you."

"It gratifies us to make friends," Han Su said.

"Terrible thing when men don't have jobs," said Slocum. "We have a few plans, but what with tomorrow being the Lord's day—"

"My husband," interrupted Han Su, "can we not promise much for everybody on Monday."

"Yes, dear. We certainly can."

Slocum told Han Su to stay put, that he was taking Fritz over to the payroll wagon. Then he put a friendly arm around Fritz's shoulders and led him a short distance away.

"Payroll wagon is right over there, Fritz. Introduce yourself to the lady inside. She's our company manager. What I actually brought you aside for is—"

"Mr. Green, I feel bound to warn you. You told the boys you'd honor Marsden script. I doubt if he'll exchange it for you. If he does, it won't be a fair dollar exchange."

"I'm sure it will all work out, Fritz. Now then, you know the wagon near where we left my wife? My brother-in-law is in it. He's—" Slocum tapped a finger against his head. "I'm leaving you the key. He's harmless, but if he should start yelling and ranting, well, you open the wagon and do what you have to."

When Slocum returned to Han Su, he found her standing with the Peshtigo chief of police. The chief had come to deliver a message. Mr. Marsden expected them at his house at nine o'clock.

The door of the white house was answered by a pretty blond girl no more than fourteen years old. She led them through the foyer, up a sweeping staircase and down a hall to Marsden's third floor office. She opened the office door and held it for them as they entered.

Marsden stood at a window, his back to them, his

large frame all but blocking out the window. His arms were folded behind his back, and his hands jutted from the sleeves of his black jacket like thick pink sausages. He spoke without turning around, his voice deep as echoing thunder.

"Serve these people a drink, Ilsa. My private stock. Then go to your room. Study your Sunday school lessons. I may want you later."

When the girl had brought them drinks, she left the office, but Marsden continued to face the window even after she had gone. Han Su stared at the man's back, her features stretched tight with hatred. She twisted her drink with such intensity Slocum feared she might break the glass. Or throw it. He saw her staring at a long steel letter opener on Marsden's desk, and he put his hand on her shoulder, indicating she should relax.

Slocum decided to play along with Marsden's waiting game. He looked at the map that covered one wall. A glancing count showed over seventy pins indicating logging camps. Fortunately, none were in the path Slocum planned to use as an escape route.

The huge steel wall safe was another matter. It was not what he had expected. It explained why Marsden kept his money here instead of in his bank. Any charge powerful enough to blow it open would also blow up the house.

Marsden finally turned, slowly, heavily, and faced them.

It was the same giant-sized figure Slocum had seen leaning from a horse that long ago night at Shiloh. But the years had softened his bulk, and he looked as if his whole, thick weight was sliding downward. His liverish eyes were nearly hidden beneath the plump flesh of his face. His gray lips drooped with a sneer expressing both contempt and ultimate power.

Slocum broke the silence. "You've a mighty pretty daughter."

"My ward," Marsden said. "The good Lord never blessed me with children of my own. It is not to me to

182

question His wisdom." He fixed Han Su with a hard stare. "You're Chinese. Good people, Chinese. I always got along well with Chinese. It's in the book, however, the races shall not cohabitate. But you are not Christians, thus do not follow the true Law. You could not be Christians and be doing what you are doing. I know why you are here."

Han Su stiffened.

"Why are we here?" Slocum asked.

Marsden grunted. "Others have tried to beat me and not gotten away with it. You won't either. See that map. That map is me! All of it! This town is me. Don't think you can come here and open a whorehouse a hundred yards outside of my town on a goddamn technicality."

"We have a legal right to establish a business on unclaimed land," said Slocum.

"Rights! Rights are what you can take. You are one man and twenty-one women out there at Schmidt's. You cannot take anything. You're too late! I came first. I took a nothing, dirt-path settlement and made it a community. I got rid of the heathen Indians and made this land a fit place for Christians to prosper and grow."

Slocum said, "We're here to prosper and grow."

"You're nothing but a godless whorehouse! You think you can make a quick killing. Whores and gambling! You think you can rape this community and ride out free and rich. You can't! I know you've a few malcontents out there tonight. You even hired that atheistic strike leader as foreman. You paid them a few dollars knowing the ignorant louts would spend it and more at your casino and whorehouse. It's an old trick, Mr. Green. Your mistake was coming here before learning most of what passed for money in this town is my company script. Now I may be willing to redeem that script, but only if you see reason! And if you don't see reason, I've my police force, I've the good Christian citizens, I've troops I can call on in Green Bay to burn you out!"

Slocum scratched his head. "You sure do talk loud and powerful considering half of your community is either on strike or out of work. That mill of yours is working at a quarter efficiency. You've logs sitting from last season, and you can't cut them because the river's too low to carry full boats. You've only ten policemen and your good Christians likely aren't good fighters. You don't want to wire Green Bay because that would mean bringing outside government into your kingdom. You let us open up tonight. You called us here to make a deal."

"I don't make deals," snorted Marsden. "I set them. You have correctly observed certain labor problems. Now, while I don't hold with whoring, I am practical and can see its temporary advantage. Your business can provide a certain entertainment to keep the men content. Therefore, I'm prepared to let you remain in business until the first snow. Could be next week, could be a month. With the first flake, you move. Naturally, there will be a tax."

"How much?" asked Han Su.

"Fifty percent."

"Never," Han Su snapped.

"Tell your Chinese wife to shut up, Green."

Slocum said, "How much will you give on the script?"

"Four bits on the dollar."

"Six," said Slocum.

"I've set the terms. Accept them or fold your tents like a goddamn Arab and get out of here."

"Do we have time to think about this?" Slocum asked.

"You've until noon tomorrow. I'll be preaching a lay sermon. You and your wife attend services and I will preach of brotherhood. If you do not, I will preach of the evils you have visited among us. When I am finished, every God-fearing man will be rushing home to pick up his rifle and march. We shall come with the fiery cross, Mr. Green, and burn you straight to hell!"

Slocum got up at dawn and saddled a horse. There was a crisp autumn nip in the air, but the sky was clear and promised a fine day. He left camp, forded the Peshtigo River and bypassed the town. He rode south about five miles to where the telegraph poles climbed up a logged-over hillside. He stopped beneath a pole, stood up on his saddle and cut the wire. Then he rode another quarter mile and cut a second line. He went a little farther and cut the line a third time.

He swung around and rode north. Again he avoided the town, but his route took him up a hill that gave a view of both Peshtigo and Schmidt's Clearing. He paused for a moment. He saw that the town was just beginning to rise to a lazy Sunday morning. Here and there he could see the smoke from a kitchen chimney. The clearing, though, still hadn't been to bed. Even at this distance he could hear the raucous noise of men having a good time.

He rode on until he came to the Indian village where Red Bear had been chief. Marsden hadn't left much standing here and it was a miserable place. All the shacks and tents where the Indians lived sagged and were beyond repair. Abandoned waste lay everywhere, leaving a foul smell. Slocum wondered why the Indians had chosen to remain here, and how they survived.

He found the new chief and showed him Red Bear's necklace and the map on which Red Bear's grandson had sketched the Indian trails.

The chief invited Slocum into his lodge, a shack in somewhat better condition than the other hovels. Slocum and the Indian squatted down on a thin reed mat. The Indian's woman brought Slocum a bowl, then left the two men alone. The bowl held a bad-tasting mixture of boiled oats-and-rice, and not until Slocum had eaten the mixture did the Indian say, "How may we help you?"

Slocum told the Indian his plans. He spoke for perhaps five minutes, during which time the Indian remained silent. When Slocum finished, the Indian stood and led Slocum back outside to his horse.

"I hope to delay the start of things until sunset," Slocum said while climbing into his saddle. "But the action could start earlier, so your men must be ready to move at any time. You'll come into the clearing and take our wagons. Drive them ten or so miles west of town and burn them. Then scatter in different directions leaving trails that will confuse the law. Myself, twenty-one women and another man will get to this village as soon as we finish our business. We need guides for your northern trails."

"It will be done," said the Indian.

It was past one o'clock by the time Slocum got back to the hill overlooking the town. The harsh clanging of bells clearly reached him. Since church should have been over an hour ago, this many bells could only mean one thing! Marsden was calling together his people. He checked his horse and watched a while. Very shortly crowds began to mass in front of the Forest House.

He rode on back to the clearing, where he was heartily cheered by nearly a thousand men. Some were pretty sorry-looking from their night of partying, others were new and fresh.

They'll do, thought Slocum with satisfaction, *they'll do just fine.*

Han Su rushed up to him as he was dismounting.

"Moy has escaped!" she said.

Fritz lay on a cot in a wagon, a crude bandage wrapped around his head. A spot of blood had soaked through the bandage, but he looked to be suffering mainly from injured dignity.

"I'm really sorry, Mr. Green," he said.

"What happened?"

Fritz frowned sheepishly. "A little feller like that getting the best of me."

"What happened?" insisted Slocum.

"It was an hour or so ago. I was passing that locked wagon. Heard one heck of a noise coming from it—sounded like an animal trying to tear it apart. So I used that key you gave me. I didn't know you had him chained up. When I seen how skinny and small he was, well, Mr. Green, for a second there I thought you was pretty inhuman. Crazy or not, a man's a man and not a dog."

"Did you release him, Fritz?"

"It did occur to me. When he first looked at me with his eyes like a thirsty bird dog, I thought of letting him go. Then his eyes went from thirsty to pure crazy, and he started yanking the chain. Heck of a noise, what with the chain and the cracking wood. Always heard crazy men got crazy strength. Never believed it until I seen him rip that chain right out of the floor."

"Goddamn," muttered Slocum. "Last I saw him, he couldn't even lift a tin cup."

"He stood there with the chain still hooked to the collar 'round his neck. Shiverin' like it was winter. No more than a third my size. Whack! He swings the chain and cracks my head, skoots by me and skedaddles like a frightened rabbit. I'm real sorry."

Slocum left Fritz. Outside, Han Su and a half-dozen girls were pacing nervously.

Slocum took Han Su aside. "This changes nothing," he said. "Notify the girls to get ready."

Han Su's voice was strained and anxious. "Moy will go to Marsden."

"He can't get near Marsden. The town is massing to come at us. They'll shoot on sight a crazy Chinaman wearing an iron collar and a chain."

Han Su refused to listen. "You must find him!"

"Moy's first thought will be breaking into a pharmacy. By the time he's well enough for any second thoughts, Marsden will be here."

"But if—"

"I can't leave now! What we wanted is about to happen."

"If Moy reaches Marsden, he will tell him who we are. Marsden may escape."

"Then we'll have to start looking for him all over again," Slocum said impatiently.

"Noooo! No!" She pounded his chest with her fists. "He cannot escape me. Not now. You must stop Moy!"

Slocum took hold of her wrists. He bent them until pain silenced her.

"Now notify the girls, Han Su. I've got to stir up the men."

He released her. She stepped back from him and looked at the marks of his hands on her wrists. "If Marsden escapes me," she hissed through tight lips, "I will kill you."

Fritz was leaning back on his cot, sipping the world's oldest cure for a headache, when Slocum returned. He looked up and apologized again for letting Moy escape.

Slocum shrugged. "How come you strikers, and most everybody else around here, have let Marsden squeeze your balls for so damn long?"

Fritz frowned. "It's his town."

"They're your balls."

Fritz's frown deepened. He swung around on the cot and put his feet on the ground and stared at his feet. "Some things you maybe don't understand, Mr. Green."

"He's wrong, you're right. What more is there to understand? Take his damn town away from him."

"Easier said, Mr. Green. He's got everybody so downhearted and poor of pocket and fighting his neighbor, well, they never have the spirit to attack him. And any man who goes at him alone gets cut down by his police."

"There's near a thousand men in our little circus

188

right now. Not a one is downhearted or fighting his neighbor."

"You think we should just march on him, huh." Fritz nodded, frowned and shook his bandaged head. "Just take everything like a band of outlaws."

"Didn't he take the land from the Indians?"

"Unless we killed him, he'd have troops here before we could change the name of his company store. We don't hold with murder."

"Last thing I want is him murdered. Man like him has to be executed. But he's massing all the so-called good people of Peshtigo to come out here and burn me out." Slocum added just a dash of derision to his voice. "I was hoping I wouldn't have to fight him alone."

Slocum turned and again left the wagon.

It had gotten hot. The midday sun felt too close to the earth. The milling crowd kicked up a thick and gritty dust, and it was difficult to breathe.

Ten girls were moving among the men, giving out bottles, laughing, teasing, hinting at a later meeting. A man received a provocative smile, perhaps a little peck on the cheek or a moment's pressure of a breast against his arm, and was left. Every girl wore boots and riding clothes beneath her long, full skirt.

A girl said to Slocum, "Better happen soon, or we're going to start dropping from the heat."

"Another hour or so," he answered. He had wanted to stretch things to sundown, but with Moy on the loose, he had decided to force the action as soon as Marsden appeared.

Fritz caught up with Slocum. "All right, Mr. Green. You've been good to us. I'll stand behind you. So will the men."

"I'm grateful, Fritz." Slocum spoke with a smile, but was not surprised. He had expected a man like Fritz would feel the need to prove his mettle after being hoodwinked by a skinny Chinaman.

"But we'll try avoiding a fight," Fritz said.

189

With Fritz's help the camp was quickly made ready and waiting for Marsden. The first couple of hours or so were filled by different men stepping forward to make speeches, each speech more impassioned than the previous one. The speakers moved from defending the rights of the circus to expressing the complaints of their community.

Then the fever came. Slocum felt it sweep over the men. Its heat overtook the heat of the day. The men began to chant the fever's name. *"Marsden. Marsden. Marsden."* Despite Fritz's constant reminders to avoid violence, Slocum noticed with no dissatisfaction that those men who had weapons were taking them out to check them.

Fritz said to Slocum, "Where is he?"

"I don't know. He should have been here by now."

"These men are getting out of hand," said Fritz.

Slocum stopped in the tent where Han Su and the other ten girls waited. They were dressed for riding. Han Su still looked like a woman, but the others had pushed their hair under their hats and done their best to clothe themselves to resemble men. Their horses were saddled and ready just outside.

"Start moving out in twos and threes the minute Marsden's people get here," Slocum said. "Moy is loose. Try to spot him before he spots you, and avoid him. I'll try to give you at least an hour to get into your positions. There'll be plenty of shots fired here. They'll sound to you like firecrackers. Wait fifteen minutes—it'll be the longest fifteen minutes of your life—then blow your safes. Grab the loot and get outside. The other girls will be waiting with the extra horses. While they're throwing the smoke bombs, load your loot on the horses. Don't wait for the other teams and don't expect to see the madame or myself. We'll be busy in the house on the hill. Soon as your team is loaded, ride out. The

Indians are waiting for you in their village. Any questions?"

One girl laughed. "We can do it blindfolded."

"I got a question," said another. "If we come on Moy while we're leaving, do we pick him up?"

"No," said Han Su.

Han Su walked beside Slocum as he made a final check on the horses. She nervously scratched an arm. "Why have they not arrived?"

"They'll come."

Slocum felt the muggy heat of the late afternoon sun. The men were feeling it, too. Their fever was leaving them. Slocum knew mobs, knew that once they lost their group fever, shame and embarrassment came over them with chilling speed.

"Moy has gotten to Marsden," insisted Han Su.

"I don't think so."

But Slocum was no longer sure. Marsden should have been here by now. Moy knew no details of the plan. He couldn't tell Marsden that ten women were going to use the cover of a riot at Schmidt's Landing to rob the safes in his bank, mill, shipping office and company store. But Moy could tell Marsden enough to make sure the man wouldn't lead his people here and leave his town unguarded.

"I should have killed Marsden last night," said Han Su. "When I had the chance."

"With your little hidden derringer?" snapped Slocum. "The slug wouldn't penetrate his fat."

"I should never have listened to you, John Slocum. Should never have trusted your plan."

Slocum looked hard at her. "I thought there was more than trust involved. But he'll get here. And I want him to stay alive until I get him to open his safe."

"I no longer care about the money."

"I do."

* * *

191

Then the townspeople came.

First was heard the growing roar of their approaching voices. They were singing.

"Onward, Christian soldiers,
Marching as to war—"

They came over a treeless ridge, the fire-and-brimstone preachers the first to appear. They were followed by a long line of people, their large number stirring the dry soil and kicking up a high swirl of dust. The flame of the setting sun sparked the dust red.

Marsden, riding a black horse, was at the center of the line. He swung a saber and also held a white cross. Spreading from either side of Marsden were his police with their sawed-off shotguns and clubs. The police were on foot, as were most of the others, who were armed with rifles, clubs, pitchforks, rocks.

"Now we know what took so long," said Fritz. "He circled around to block you from riding west. He knows your wagons can't ford the river. He must want your wagons."

"He can't have them," said Han Su.

"Well," said Slocum. "Let's go greet him."

Slocum, Han Su and Fritz stood in front of the men from the clearing and watched the steady, though unhurried, approach of the singing townspeople. The men were quiet, but it was a tense and restless quiet, and Slocum felt their tension. He knew it wouldn't take much to set them off.

Marsden halted his horse six yards from them; the townspeople stopped with him and their singing voices went silent. Marsden remained on his horse, and it occurred to Slocum that the huge man on the black horse truly looked like a vengeful Old Testament patriarch. Marsden lifted his white cross from a scabbard attached to his saddle; its shaft was sharpened to a point.

"Lord in heaven!" shouted Marsden. "We proudly serve you."

He raised the cross high for a moment, then flung it, and it stabbed into the ground near Slocum's feet.

"Hallelujah!" cried the preachers.

"Hallelujah!" chorused Marsden's people.

"The forces of righteousness are here!" Marsden's voice boomed over the chorusing shouts of the townspeople. "We have come to remove the stain of your whorehouse, Green."

"You're removing nothing," said Slocum. "Least of all a whorehouse. Look at these men behind me. How could I have a whorehouse and satisfy all of them with only twenty girls?"

Marsden pointed his saber down at Slocum. "You saddle up and leave peaceably. Leave your wagons. We're claiming them as your punishment."

"Wagons are our private property," said Han Su.

"Those who disobey God's laws must be punished!"

"Could it be," shouted Fritz, "that God needs Mr. Green's wagons to haul Marsden Company freight?"

The men in the clearing responded loudly to Fritz's remark. They hooted and cheered and yelled obscenities, and then the fire-and-brimstone preacher began pounding his drum and all the townspeople shouted and added to the din.

"Listen to me," hollered Marsden. He threw his arms into the air and waved his saber, amazingly causing everybody to grow quiet. "I know every last one of you louts in that clearing. Step aside! Or by heaven none of you will ever work for Marsden Company again."

A man called, "We ain't worked in some while now."

"Nor been paid honest cash either," yelled another.

"Green pays cash," yelled a third. "And he's promised work for all tomorrow."

"You take his word?" sneered Marsden. "The word of a man who would marry a yellow-skinned woman. The Scriptures forbid such an alliance!"

Fritz said, "What do the Scriptures say about you and Hans Muller's orphaned daughter?"

Marsden rose up in his saddle. "Mister, are you implying—"

"You rape that little girl," shouted Fritz. "You rape her whenever you take the notion. Everybody knows it. The shame of Peshtigo is letting you get away with it!"

"Lies! Lies!" Marsden swung around to his people. "Sing, my brethren. Shout down the devil's voice with song. Sing! And we shall march over these people." He pumped his saber up and down and began to lead them in song.

> *"Mine eyes have seen the glory of*
> *the coming of the Lord,*
> *He is trampling out the vin—"*

The rumble of an explosion was heard. It sounded like distant thunder, but it wasn't thunder and it caught the attention of both crowds. Slocum and Han Su exchanged a glance, and Han Su said to him, "It's too soon." Then came a second explosion, followed by a third.

"Look to the heavens!" shouted Marsden. "It thunders! The Lord has loosed upon us His thunder and rain. He shows us His favor."

But the crowd wasn't looking to the heavens. The crowd was looking back toward Peshtigo. And at the black smoke bellowing into the darkening sky, and the rising red glow beneath the smoke.

"Fire!"

It was the panicked shriek of all their voices.

There was another explosion, the loudest yet, and a streak of flame blazed into the air.

Suddenly there were no opposing sides. All rushed toward town, dropping their weapons as they ran. They ran to save their families, their homes. All feared they had already been burned out. None had ever seen a fire explode so high so fast, and they ran sick with their fear, and they all knew, no matter their own loss, they would have to work together to stop the fire before it spread to the forest, the drought dry, dry-as-tinder forest.

Slocum and Han Su and the girls were soon alone in the camp. The girls looked to Slocum for orders.

"Tear off those heavy dresses," ordered Slocum. "We're riding."

Han Su gripped his arm. "Marsden is getting away!"

Slocum pushed her aside and went to a girl who was clumsily fumbling with the hooks of her dress. He took hold of the dress and ripped it off her.

"I said tear the damn things! Don't waste time."

"What went wrong?" asked the girl.

"Our charges weren't heavy enough to make those explosions," Slocum answered. "But we're riding in."

The girl trembled. "If the forest catches, we'll never get out alive."

"Mount up!" called Slocum. "We got ten people to get out of there. If we can still get some money, we'll damn well take it, too."

The girls hesitated. A few mounted their horses, but none made the least move to spur her animal.

"There's no wind," said Slocum. "Fire won't reach the forest without a wind to push it."

Suddenly, one of those girls who had been sent ahead raced into the clearing. She looked like a wild thing, her clothing filthy, her face streaked with sweat and soot. She pulled her horse to a halt and yelled, "Moy! He's bombing and torching the whole damn town."

Han Su lashed out, "I told you! John Slocum."

Slocum ignored her. "Where are the rest of our people?" he asked the girl.

"Blowin' safes! Couldn't get in the company store. All the rest we're taking. Sent me to make sure you were coming."

Slocum leaped onto his horse while saying, "Where's the fire at now?"

"Both sides of the river. Lot of little fires on the business side. Over on the other, where all them shacks and piecemeal houses were, that's one big blaze. It's all

195

spreadin' fast. We got about thirty minutes to get in and out if we don't want blistered asses."

"We can do it in twenty." Slocum turned to the others. "Well? You going to leave them there to roast?"

22

Slocum stopped them a hundred yards from the outskirts of town. The heat was already hot against their flesh. Sparks flew above. Some landed near on the ground and continued to burn as coals. His horse whinnied and pulled at its bridle.

"Tear some cloth," he ordered the girls. "Soak it down with your canteens. Wrap a smoke cover over your nose and mouths and blindfold your horses. We'll have to lead them from here on."

The girls set to work. Han Su came up to him as he was blindfolding his horse.

"The house on the hill is safe from all flames," she said.

"Is your horse blindfolded, Han Su?"

"I am going to his house."

"Go ahead. But he's in town trying to save what he's got there."

"Then I go with you."

He took hold of her arm as she started away, spun her around and slapped her.

She gasped, "I told you never to strike me."

Slocum nodded. "We've people in that furnace. We put them there, and we're going to get them out. Then you and I can get Marsden. When the fire starts crawling up his hill, he'll rush home and open his safe to get his money. That's when we take him."

"Perhaps you are right." She threw her arms around him and pressed her body close. She felt remarkably cool. "Do not lose faith in me."

It was, thought Slocum, more a command than a request.

He led them on. The heat against his face became hotter. A gust of breeze had carried the increased heat. He shouted over his shoulder, "You girls who were on the team for the company store switch to the mill. Rest of you follow original plans."

"What if we get cut off?" asked a girl.

"Head for the river and wait it out."

There was another explosion as they entered town. One whole side of the mill went up like a torch. Slocum and Han Su headed there with five girls.

They had to lead their horses. People charging every which way jammed the streets. Rubble and burning debris lay everywhere; the air was thick with smoke.

The firefighters were working with buckets and blankets and spades. They had given up on many buildings and were trying to stop the fire from spreading. Some were on the roofs, covering them with wet blankets and shawls. Others used spades of dirt and blankets to beat at the flames that curled along the wooden sidewalks.

"Watch for Moy," Slocum told Han Su. "Got to stop him."

Women with children in their arms were desperately seeking shelter. They ran blindly with wet aprons covering their faces. One ran past Slocum, unaware of the flame licking up the hem of her dress.

Slocum thrust the reins of his horse at Han Su. "Don't lose our horses."

He chased the woman and pushed her down. He threw himself over her and smothered the flames. The woman's baby cried; she stumbled to her feet and ran on. A bone-shattering screech came from behind Slocum. He spun around. A crazed mule was bearing down on him, yellow teeth snapping, hooves kicking.

A firefighter knocked Slocum aside. "That carriage!" the firefighter yelled. "Give me a hand!"

Slocum helped the man pull a burning carriage from beneath the overhanging balcony of the Forest House. They left it in the center of the street, and Slocum

197

worked his way back to Han Su. Together they made it to the mill. The town's only fire engine was there, and Marsden was giving orders. A bucket brigade passed water from the river to keep the engine pump's cistern filled. Four men worked the pump; Marsden directed others as to where to aim the spray from the hose.

"Pull 'em boys!" shouted Marsden. "Pull those pumps."

At the side of the mill the pyramid stacks of logs were beginning to catch. As the stakes holding the pyramids gave way, the logs rolled into the river. People who had sought refuge in the river struggled desperately to avoid the logs that rolled down at them. Across the river all was ablaze with high flames. The water shimmered as if it, too, had taken fire, while the forest beyond rocked and tossed. Slocum knew it was only a matter of time—a short time—before the forest caught.

A figure appeared on the roof of the mill.

"Look!" went up the cry. "It's a woman!"

Han Su gripped Slocum's arm. "It's one of our girls."

Men ran forward with a stretched-out blanket, going dangerously close to the burning mill, and yelled for her to jump. The fire was so loud, it was doubtful the woman was able to hear them, and if she jumped there was no chance the blanket would break her fall.

"Save the mill," ordered Marsden. "Save it, you save her."

"He's right," said Slocum. But before he could lend a hand, a muffled explosion came from inside the building. It shook the burning walls, and the windows on the upper story shattered and sent out a shower of glass shards. The walls of the mill began to fall, slowly at first, then with increasing speed. Slocum grabbed Han Su, pulling her out of the path of the collapsing front wall, but the firemen who had tried to drag their engine to safety were trapped.

There was a shout. "The river's burning!"

198

The crashing mill had spilled drums of oil into the river. The oil had ignited and now a sheet of flame licked over the water. Han Su pressed her hands to her ears. Nothing could shut out the screams that came from those trapped in the river.

"It is hopeless," said Han Su. But then her eyes widened and she thrust out an arm. "There! Moy! He ran into the alley of the Forest House."

"Stay here," Slocum said. He charged up the street, brutally throwing aside anybody or anything blocking his way, and threw himself against the wall of the hotel. He cautiously leaned around the corner of the building and looked up the alley. He saw nobody.

He entered the alley. It was darker here between the buildings. Red shadows lit his way as he ran to the far corner of the hotel. He heard laughter coming from just around the corner. Moy was laughing hysterically. Slocum drew his gun and rounded the corner.

Moy was on his hands and knees digging around inside a crate. He spotted Slocum and jumped to his feet, a glass jar in his hand. The chain that still hung from his iron collar glistened. His eyes were glassy.

"Ahhhh! Mr. Green. No. I shall call you Slocum."

"You know what you've caused?" muttered Slocum.

"I have assisted my beloved cousin in sacking the town of Peshtigo." He held the glass jar high. "Is it not wondrous what modern pharmacies make available. My ancestors worked centuries to perfect what I manufactured in minutes. Shoot me and this jar shall blow you up as I fall."

"I'll shoot you and catch it before you fall."

"You are not so quick. Put away your gun."

"And then?"

"I throw the jar that way or this way. And you and I have it out once and for ended."

"You insane sonofa—for God's sake think of the innocent women and children."

"They are not my women and children," laughed

199

Moy. He swung back his arm, as if to throw the jar. Slocum lunged to try and stop him, but Moy made a twisting little half-step and danced in toward Slocum. The momentum of his lunge kept Slocum from stopping and he saw Moy's chain snake out at him. Moy was using the chain as he had used his pigtail. It smashed hard into Slocum's face, stunning him. He fell.

Moy quickly put aside the jar. Slocum lay dazed and Moy had no trouble kicking the gun from Slocum's hand. Moy giggled and laughed. He reached into a sleeve and produced a cleaver.

"You see, Slocum! See how well equipped are pharmacies. Now I split your head." He raised the cleaver and prepared to throw it. "First I split it. Then I hack it into tiny pieces."

"No, my cousin." Han Su's voice came from the corner of the alley. "You will harm no one ever again." She held her derringer in her hand.

"You will not shoot," said Moy. "You will not kill me, the last of your family. Me, the man who stood loyally by you despite your deceits."

The derringer made almost no noise as she fired it. A red hole appeared in Moy's forehead. His cleaver dropped from his hands as he reeled backward, and he raised his hands as if trying to reach the red hole. His hands never made it. He crashed against a garbage barrel and slid lifelessly to the ground.

Han Su rushed to Slocum. "Quickly," she said, "Marsden just rode away in the direction of his house."

The fire sizzled and scorched the short grass around their feet as they rushed up the hill. They were on foot. Han Su had lost their horses when she followed Slocum into the alley. Flames had reached the trees behind Marsden's house and the back of the house had started to burn. Beneath them, Peshtigo was an inferno.

Marsden's horse kicked at the hitching post in front of the house. Marsden hadn't bother to blindfold it, and the animal struggled to loosen itself, its black body awash with gray sweat. It was too caught up in panic or Slocum would have tried to calm it down. It would have come in handy for their getaway.

The front door of the house stood open. They went in, and Slocum had to stop Han Su from running recklessly up the stairs. He pushed her behind him, drew his gun, and they started up the stairs, slowly, one step at a time.

They heard a shatter of glass when they reached the first floor landing. It came from the rear of the house.

"Heat pressure," Slocum said quietly. "The fire's broken through and is inside the house."

They continued up the stairs. They heard the noise of the fire spreading below them. Slocum had to take hold of Han Su, because she kept trying to charge ahead too fast. Smoke began to drift up and twist around their legs as they reached the third floor. They turned onto the corridor and moved on to Marsden's office.

The door was ajar. Slocum leaned forward and looked through the opening. The wide, steel door of the safe was open. Marsden was shuffling about in the glow from a single small lamp burning on his desk. Near the lamp were two satchels. He was pulling handfuls of money from his safe and stuffing it into the satchels.

Slocum pushed into the room. "We'll take over from here, Marsden."

"What right have you to—" Then Marsden noticed Slocum's gun. He slowly raised his arms into the air.

Han Su moved forward. "Kill him, John Slocum." A thin sheen of sweat covered her face. Her lips were drawn tight.

"Slocum?" Marsden growled. "Thought your name was Green."

"Kill him!"

"Not yet, Han Su. First he's got to know why he's being killed."

201

"What the hell is this?" spouted Marsden. "Who are you people?"

"I am Han Su Lu." She went closer to Marsden and spat in his face.

"Don't block my way," warned Slocum.

"I don't know you," sneered Marsden.

Han Su picked up the lamp and held it near her face. She was shaking; emotion caused her voice to crack. "I was but fourteen. I was your animal. By day you killed my people; at night you violated me. I have lived for this moment, lived to watch you die like the—" She broke down and began to weep.

Marsden looked at Slocum. "Woman's got me confused with someone."

"Marsden's Treachery," said Slocum.

"Never heard of it," Marsden answered.

"Friends of mine, and a lot of other good men, were massacred because you weren't allowed to assume Johnson's command after Shiloh. Hundreds of men, all horribly slaughtered. I wish there wasn't a fire coming up the stairs, Marsden. I wish I had time to kill you slowly."

"I served my nation as an officer and a gentle—"

Slocum fired a shot that creased Marsden's fat cheek.

"You want money?" Marsden cautiously touched his wounded cheek. "Take it. Enough for all of us. More in the safe. More than I can carry."

"We take all," said Han Sun.

"Then what?" Marsden's voice boomed out as if he weren't under the point of a gun. "Then what, you yellow-skinned bitch? How you going to get away? You're surrounded by fire."

"Give me the gun, John Slocum." She moved toward Slocum. The small lamp in her hand lit her features with a fierce light. "Give me! I will kill him myself."

"Want to live?" boomed Marsden. "Help me carry my money. I got a boat waiting."

Han Su tried to grab Slocum's gun. He pulled back, but she managed to get a hold on his arm and struggled with him for the gun. Marsden took advantage of the moment. He reached into one of his satchels and pulled out a Colt. Slocum was still struggling with Han Su when Marsden fired two shots. She screamed as a bullet shattered her spine, and Marsden swung around and hid behind the steel door of his safe.

Han Su slumped against Slocum, loosening her grip on his arm. He kept Marsden busy by firing off a round that clanged against the steel door, and he gently lowered her to the floor. He whispered her name. She tried to respond but was unable to speak. Her eyes clouded and closed, her head flopped to the side, and in her dying moment she managed to weakly throw the lamp which she had somehow held onto.

The lamp rolled across the floor and broke against Marsden's desk. The oil splashed a line of blue flame along the floor, and Slocum began to edge back as Marsden fired a blind shot from behind the steel door. The bullet missed Slocum by yards.

He dropped low behind a chair near a window. He stayed quiet, waiting for Marsden to make a move. The office rapidly filled with smoke from the burning house, and the line of fire created by the broken lamp was growing. One end licked the base of Marsden's desk; the other had nearly reached the opposite wall.

"You're a dead man, Slocum," Marsden called. "Surrender to me. I'll save you."

"Why would you save me?"

"Need two to carry all my money. Help me get it to the boat. I'll give you a ride out of here."

"Your river's on fire and full of smoke. Nobody could navigate it."

"I got the best captain, the best of instruments. He'll get us out."

The fire in the office continued to grow. The floorboards had caught. Marsden's wall map was beginning to crackle with inching flames.

"Throw me your weapon, Slocum."

Through the office door, Slocum saw that the fire in the house had reached the corridor. The only exit left was the window behind him.

"Look around, Marsden. You're the one who's trapped."

Suddenly, flame burst into the office from the corridor. The fire already there shot higher and the separate fires rushed to meet. The wall with Marsden's map gushed with flame. The little flags sizzled on their pins, and the pins popped loose.

"Look at your map, Marsden," shouted Slocum. "There goes your empire."

The ceiling started to burn. The heat was increasing with each moment and Slocum backed nearer to the window. He touched the glass, searing his fingers; he crouched low. The steel safe was shimmering with a bright orange glow and Slocum knew Marsden couldn't hold out much longer.

"Slocum!" Marsden shouted. "Any deal you want. But let's get out of here!"

Slocum answered with a shot.

"You want the money? You can have it all!"

Slocum fired again. He cupped a hand over his forehead to shield his eyes from the heat and watched the flames burn nearer and nearer Marsden.

"God in heaven, Slocum! Have mercy!"

The ceiling beams cracked and dripped fire.

"*Sloc—!*"

Marsden lunged from behind the steel door, his huge body sheathed in flame. He pitched past Slocum and crashed through the window.

Slocum climbed onto the windowsill. He glanced at the desk. The money was just another fire. He looked at the ground below and jumped. As his heels touched down, he curled his knees against his face, then tumbled down the hill. When he came to a stop, he got to his feet and found he was midway between the inferno at the foot of the hill and the blazing forest. There was nothing left to burn on the hill. The buckle of his belt was hot in his hands as he pulled the belt out and began digging at the earth, using the buckle as a scoop. In the midst of his digging a tremendous explosion shook the ground, and he looked up to see a huge orange fireball rising into the sky. The heat had become such that the forest was blowing itself up. Slocum felt himself quake as he watched the awesome fireball rise. He went back to his digging. He dug a hole the size of a shallow grave. Flaming branches were falling all around him as he dropped into his hole, wrapping his shirt over his face and clawing at the dirt until he had buried himself.

The earth continued to shake. For a long time he heard over the roar of fire the agonized shrieks of Marsden's horse still tied to the hitching post.

Twenty-four hours after it began, the Peshtigo Fire came to an end when the scorched sky let loose rain.

23

Slocum stood at the Battery tip of Manhattan Island smoking a cigar and watching the sun spill over the eastern horizon. He was tired. He had just walked out of a card game, leaving it while in the middle of a winning streak; he was considering whether it was worth it to drag himself back to his hotel to collect the few things he had there.

He'd been in New York a week. He had spent nearly all the time searching the Chinese quarter for the man to whom Han Su had said she was sending their money. Yesterday afternoon he had finally located the man on a dim back street of Chinatown.

The man was very old. He was sitting in the back of a restaurant drinking tea from a small cup without a handle. He was dressed as opulently as Moy had dressed, and he was surrounded by a number of men wearing gray city suits. He dismissed the men with a wave of his hand, nodded for Slocum to sit down, and poured Slocum a cup of tea.

"You have been looking for me."

"Yes," said Slocum. He told the man why he had come.

"I see," the old man said with a nod. "I was to hold in trust a sum of money sent me from Chicago. But, as you know, Chicago has suffered a tragic fire. The express offices were all destroyed."

"This would have gone out before the fire."

"And how large was this sum?"

"Approximately three-quarters of a million dollars."

"A large sum to entrust to a stranger."

"Madame Lu told me she knew you."

The old man smiled. "She knew of me. As I knew of her. What I control here, she, in her small way, controlled in the west. Had I received her money, I would have guarded it. For a small fee, of course. However, I did not receive it. And I can assure you, sir, no such large sum has been received by anyone within this community."

The old man could have been lying, but Slocum didn't think so. He thanked the old man for giving the courtesy of his time, and then he had gone out and bought into the first high-stakes poker game he could find.

He took a final puff on his cigar and threw it into the waters of the Hudson River.

"Han Su."

He said her name aloud. There was a smile on his face as he said it, but there was no tone to his voice, no high or low, no emotion.

He turned from the river and started walking away. His boot heels clicked against cement. He didn't like the sound of cement under his heels and he walked faster, heading toward the train station in the center of the city.

He smiled.

In a few minutes a train was pulling out and heading west. He would be on it.

OTHER JAKE LOGAN WESTERNS
FEATURING THAT NOTORIOUS
HELL-BENT-FOR-TROUBLE VARMINT
JOHN SLOCUM

ORDER DIRECTLY FROM:
PLAYBOY PRESS
P.O. Box 3585
Chicago, Illinois 60654

No. of copies		Title	Price
_____	B16282	Hanging Justice	$1.25
_____	B16281	Ride, Slocum, Ride	1.25
_____	B16287	Slocum and the Widow Kate	1.25
_____	B16293	Across the Rio Grande	1.25
_____	B16301	The Comanche's Woman	1.25
_____	B16308	Slocum's Gold	1.25
_____	B16318	Bloody Trail to Texas	1.25
_____	B16338	North to Dakota	1.25
_____	B16356	Slocum's Woman	1.25
_____	B16375	White Hell	1.25
_____	B16394	Ride for Revenge	1.25
_____	B16416	Outlaw Blood	1.25
_____	B16434	Montana Showdown	1.25
_____	B16458	See Texas and Die	1.25
_____	B16475	Iron Mustang	1.25
_____	B16493	Slocum's Blood	1.25

Please enclose 50¢ for postage and handling if one book i ordered, 75¢ if two to five are ordered. If six or more ar ordered, postage is free. No cash, CODs or stamps. Send chec or money order, or charge your Playboy Club Credit Key #

_____

Total amount enclosed: $_____

Name _____

Address _____

City _____ State _____ Zip _____